Open Your Eyes

KINGS GROVE - BOOK TWO

by Delancey Stewart

Copyright © 2018 Delancey Stewart
All rights reserved.

OPEN YOUR EYES by Delancey Stewart
All rights reserved. Published in the United States of America.

No part of this book may be used or reproduced in any manner whatsoever without written permission of the publisher, except in the case of brief quotations embodied in critical articles and reviews.

OPEN YOUR EYES is a work of fiction. Names, characters, places, and incidents are either products of the author's imagination or are used fictitiously. Any resemblance to actual persons, living or dead, business establishments, events, or locales is entirely coincidental.

This book was originally published as LOVE REIMAGINED.

Contents

Chapter 1	1
Chapter 2	6
Chapter 3	10
Chapter 4	18
Chapter 5	20
Chapter 6	29
Chapter 7	35
Chapter 8	40
Chapter 9	50
Chapter 10	62
Chapter 11	71
Chapter 12	82
Chapter 13	88
Chapter 14	95
Chapter 15	101
Chapter 16	105
Chapter 17	117
Chapter 18	119
Chapter 19	126
Chapter 20	131
Chapter 21	141
Chapter 22	154
Chapter 23	163
Chapter 24	170
Chapter 25	174
Chapter 26	181
Chapter 27	183
Chapter 28	196
Chapter 29	199
Epilogue	208

Also by Delancey Stewart

Chapter 1

MIRANDA

"Remember, it's all about getting the corners lined up." My mother's voice floated toward me when I walked into the house, and my stomach clenched.

Oh God. I thought we'd gotten past this.

"Just flip that second corner over the first one on your right hand." She giggled maniacally after this line. I could deliver this entire thing from heart, getting every single inflection exactly right, I'd heard it so many times.

"Mom, not again." I walked into the living room to find Mom standing in front of the television, a fitted sheet dangling from her hands and tears running down her face. On the television in front of her, she stood in exactly the same position, a brighter, younger version of herself. "I thought you'd made peace with this."

She gave me an apologetic shrug and turned back to the television, where her younger self was just beginning to run into trouble.

"It's just this third corner that is always so difficult, but I promise you, everyone—once you get this one, it all just falls into place. You'll have beautifully folded sheets from now on and that linen closet will finally be neat and orderly." A false brightness had crept into TV Mom's voice, along with a sharp edge of panic. I hated watching this part.

"Mom, we should turn this off." I walked to the television and reached to stop the DVR, but Mom stopped me.

"No, I need to see it. I just ..." As Mom's TV self started to flail miserably and blush furiously while she tried time and again to fold that bright red fitted sheet into submission on *Wake Up Kings Grove*, real-life Mom had folded her sheet into a perfectly tidy little square. "How could I have done that?" Mom asked me, setting the sheet on the coffee table and patting it. She sank to the couch. "How did it go so wrong?"

I sat down beside her, dropping my keys on top of her sheet. We watched the rest together, painful as it was.

"Maybe if you try again, slowly?" Angela Sugar, the host of King's Grove's morning show was trying to help TV Mom fold the sheet. "I'm sure you do this all the time successfully ...

Mom snapped, "I do!" Her voice was high and warbly. "I do this all the time. I'm a professional goddamn organizer. What is wrong with me?" The sheet that filled the TV screen almost blocked out Angela's shocked face, but not quite.

The segment was nearing its awful end, my mother next to me wracked with silent sobs. "It ruined me," she was moaning. "It was supposed to launch my business, and instead I'm the organizing laughing stock."

"You're overreacting." She wasn't, really. The last part of the segment, where Mom began to flip out and her face turned bright red as she flung the sheet this way and that, had gone viral on the Internet not long after it aired. Her desperate attempts to demonstrate how easy it was to fold a fitted sheet became a meme that had even popped up on my Facebook feed. And since half of Mom's business revolved around her blog, it didn't take long for her to catch wind of it. When that happened, she definitely overreacted. I thought it would have been great if she'd owned it, and used her flub to promote her business—"Even a professional organizer struggles to get things in order sometimes ... "—something like that. But Mom had tried to pretend it never happened. Except at home, where she watched the segment on endless repeat, practicing the skill that had "ruined" her. Our linen closet was extremely tidy.

"You can turn it off," she sniffed as TV Mom ran from the stage, the sheet bundled in her arms and her wailing voice following behind her as Angela smiled into the camera with wide what-just-happened? eyes.

"No, I like this next part," I said. I put an arm around her and patted her shoulder. Angela introduced the next guest.

"President of Palmer Construction, and the man who's singlehandedly saving the Kings Grove campground cottages ... Please help me welcome Chance Palmer!"

My heart raced as gorgeous Chance Palmer strode confidently across the stage to give Angela a warm hug. His dark hair was waved over his forehead, cut short around the sides, and the perfect teeth showed as he smiled at her with a warmth I envied. He arranged his long limbs into the chair next to her and looked out into the camera. This was the part where I always pretended Chance was looking out at me, smiling that perfect smile at *me*.

Angela leaned in when Chance got close and tried to share a knowing giggle with him as my mother's wailing cry floated back onto the set, but Chance shook his head. "You know, I cannot fold one of those for the life of me. I usually end up in tears, too," he said. "I think I'm going to call Esther to come take a look at my linen closet. It's a disaster ..." He smiled and there was something so sincere about him I had no doubt every person watching fell in love with him just a little bit right then. I fell in love with him a little more every time I watched him try to make my mother's humiliation just a little bit less horrid.

Angela was clearly won over. She smiled a moony smile at

him. "Tell us about this latest project, Chance. Is it true you're renovating the Kings Grove cottages out of the goodness of your heart?"

Chance laughed, his low honeyed voice stirring something in my blood to life. I was warm all over as he began to speak. "I don't know that I'd put it that way, Angela. Those cottages are part of our history—Kings Grove history. They've stood for almost a hundred years, and I just can't stomach the state of disrepair they've fallen into. Palmer Construction has a not-for-profit foundation in addition to our primary business—and this is just the latest project for the Foundation."

"That's wonderful, Chance. You're really preserving a piece of Kings Grove history then, aren't you?"

Chance nodded, a lock of dark hair falling across his forehead. "That's the idea," he said. "My great grandparents came up here as visitors in the early 1900s, and these big trees got under their skin and they stayed. I know lots of folks now who come up here as guests every summer, and those cottages are part of their experience, their family memory. I want to be sure that future generations will have the same opportunity—if not to live up here, then to have a way to visit every year."

I'd fallen into a kind of trance, watching Chance Palmer in the unguarded way I wanted to stare at him in real life. In front of the television I could study him, notice the way the fine lines crinkled at the corners of his eyes, focus on how he lifted his chin just so when he made a point. I could stare at him forever. But when he came into the diner where I worked, I could barely form two words, and I usually spilled something on him just to seal the deal.

"Miranda." Mom was staring at me.

When Chance's segment ended, I turned to face her, eyebrows up in question.

"Honey, enough. You can't stay up here your whole life

mooning over that boy and working in a diner. Look what's become of me."

"I think you're being a little dramatic. Besides, I'm working on my degree. And then I'll decide what to do."

She shook her head. "Interior design isn't something folks need a lot of in the mountains, honey."

"Maybe I can start a blog, make a living like you do."

Dad had wandered through the living room, eating a sandwich, and overheard this last part. "She used to make a living," he said. "But since Sheetgate ..." He grinned.

Mom began to cry again.

I stood. I'd had enough. "I've got work, guys. Are you coming in for dinner tonight?" My folks liked to eat at the diner once a week when I was working.

Dad nodded. His olive green uniform was covered in dust. "Just gotta get cleaned up."

"You're a mess, Dad."

"It's so dry out there," he said. "There are just clouds of dust floating around the trails in some places—especially if you run into horses." Dad was a park ranger, and he spent his days working at the visitor center, leading hikes, and working on the trails around the National Park.

I grabbed my Kings Grover Diner shirt and headed back out the door.

"See you at the diner!"

Chapter 2

SAM

"Chance, I'll see you at the office," I called behind me as I opened the front door of the house I'd lived in since I'd been born.

"See you," he called back, lifting a coffee cup my way and staring down at his phone. "You stopping by Carolynn Teague's place? She called the office three times yesterday." He looked up and grinned at me.

I blew out a breath and gave him a level look. "Yes."

His grin spread wider. "Got a ladder?" He was enjoying this too much.

"I have the ladder. I'm just going to go fix her imaginary leak, and then I'll be in."

He chuckled and returned his gaze to his phone. "Have fun, Sam. Don't let her get you as you climb down …"

It was a valid warning. Mrs. Teague had what might have been described as 'a thing' for me; she called me out to her cabin at least once every two weeks to repair shingles that weren't broken, patch pipes that hadn't burst, and rehang doors that were perfectly hung. It was our thing. And I put up with it for two reasons—one, Mrs. Teague was a nice old lady, even if she did get a little handsy now and then; and two—she always paid for the work.

Today I found myself climbing up to the roof, Mrs. Teague insisting that she needed to 'hold the ladder' as I went up. I could feel her eyes boring holes into my butt as I climbed above her, but she was mostly harmless, so I just swallowed hard and hustled to the top. With a normal job, I'd send one of the guys out, but Mrs. Teague had been asking for me specifically since high school, and I'd been coming down here to help her long enough to know the whole situation was benign.

"Right up here, Mrs. Teague?" I called down, choosing a random spot on her perfectly intact shingled roof to repair.

She had stepped out a few feet, so she had a perfect view of me as I knelt on her sloped roof. I smiled down at her while simultaneously trying to make sure I didn't slide off. Death wasn't on my agenda today. "That's perfect, Sam," she called up. "My, you're so strong and capable."

Working for Mrs. Teague should have been an ego boost. She definitely appreciated my, uh, assets. And it was nice to hear sometimes, but the compliments would have been more appreciated coming from someone else. Specifically Miranda George, who I was pretty sure hadn't actually looked at me since we were six. Miranda had decided about then that she was in love with my older brother Chance, and while everyone said we look alike, Miranda didn't seem to share that opinion, or she just didn't care. I doubted she'd really ever even noticed the similarities, because she was too blinded by Chance and his glittering perfection. Chance was all charm and personality. I was … well, I was just me.

"Yep, I think I've got it just about patched up here," I called down to Mrs. Teague.

"Was it a big hole, Sam?"

"Big enough," I lied, hammering in a fresh shingle to replace the perfectly good one I'd removed. "This ought to do it." I scooted back down the roof toward the ladder, tucking my hammer into the tool belt at my waist.

"Oh, careful now!" She called up, and I could tell that she'd moved back to 'hold the ladder' for me again. I swallowed my pride and climbed down, wishing she'd take a few steps back as my butt ended up pretty much in her face at the bottom.

It was a surprisingly hot morning, and sweat was already beading on my forehead. I wiped at it and rolled up my sleeves when I hit the ground. Mrs. Teague's appreciative eyes followed every motion.

"Iced tea, Sam?" She smiled sweetly at me.

"That's awfully nice of you, Mrs. Teague, but I need to get on into work. My brother will be expecting me," I told her.

She nodded and continued smiling at me. "You boys work so hard," she said. "All that hammering and nailing and … drilling." She blushed and I tried not to cringe, turning instead to pull down the ladder and get it hooked back to the truck.

Chance and I didn't do a lot of actual construction at this point, hiring out crews for most of the labor, but she didn't need to be corrected. Mrs. Teague was all by herself up here, and I didn't really mind dropping by now and then if it made her … happy.

"Okay, well," I said, pulling my keys from my pocket. "I think we're all set here. You take care, Mrs. Teague, and give me a call when you need me." I dropped one arm over the old lady's shoulder and leaned down to kiss her cheek. She giggled and grinned like a girl, blushing furiously.

"Thank you, Sam," she said. Her voice was breathy and high, and her eyes didn't leave me as I climbed into the truck and gave her a final wave.

I got back to the office a few minutes later, and Chance

called out as I came through the front door, "Did you get out of there okay, little bro? Chastity intact?"

"Shut up." I threw my bag into the corner of my office and sat down at my desk. I guessed that was one of the differences between Chance and me. He would never have gotten into a situation like the one I was in with Mrs. Teague because he would have charmed and avoided. And I would never get out of it because I didn't have that skill set. I was pretty much just me—what you see is what you get. And I didn't have it in me to disappoint little old ladies.

Chapter 3
MIRANDA

The familiar smell of bacon grease and Pine-Sol greeted me as I flew through the diner door, Adele on guard at the podium to shake her head at me as always. I knew deep down she really liked me, but she did her best to hide it.

"Twelve minutes late," she said.

I gave her a grin and went to the back to clock in. There was no point arguing with Adele. She and her husband Frank owned the diner, and had run it as long as I'd been there—Adele with a firm hand and Frank with a soft smile.

"Hey you." Maddie Turner greeted me when I came back out, a pot of coffee in her hand and a smile on her face. Behind her, her fiancé Connor shot a hand up in greeting before returning to the laptop on the table in front of him.

"Hey yourself," I said. "Busy?" I looked around at the almost-full restaurant.

Maddie nodded. "Yeah, it's nice to see things picking up after such a slow winter."

"Winter's always slow up here," I told her. "Even when there's no snow." And there hadn't been more than a couple feet this year—nothing like the snowfalls I remembered growing up. We had pictures from my childhood of me standing on the roof of the house while Dad dug a tunnel down to the door. In those photos, the house was so buried it looked like a log or a boulder under feet of soft snow—not like a two-story house. We hustled around until lunchtime, getting only a slight break before the midday crowd began trickling in.

Maddie's eyes had landed on someone just over my shoulder and then she whispered, "Your table."

I turned to see Chance Palmer and his brother Sam standing at Adele's podium, looking around the crowded restaurant. Adele sat them in Maddie's section.

"Go ahead," Maddie urged.

My head spun every time I saw Chance. He was gorgeous when I watched him trying to make up for my mom's humiliation on television, but that had been a year ago. He was even better looking in real life. I'd thought so since high school, and heaven knew he'd only improved with age. Both brothers looked like they'd been working hard, their work shirts rolled up to the elbow and dusty jeans brushing the tops of steel-toed work boots.

I took a deep breath. I could do this.

I walked to their table, order pad in hand, and celebrated a minor victory when I arrived without tripping. "Hey guys." My voice was higher than I would've liked. I cleared my throat and pushed my glasses up my nose. "What can I get you to drink?"

Both brothers turned to look at me, and two sets of deep blue-gray eyes made me feel like I was under a microscope.

"Hey Miranda, how's it going?" Chance said and then turned his attention back to his menu.

"Good," I managed, trying to force my voice to remain in one octave.

Sam's eyes stayed on my face, and I wished he would return to his menu, too. Sam Palmer had never been my favorite person and he wasn't my favorite Palmer brother by a long shot. "How's school?" he asked.

I shrugged, waving the order pad in front of me. "Fine. I still have a ways to go."

"Probably get more done if you weren't hanging out in a diner." He cleared his throat. "I mean, you'd have more time for school."

"Iced tea, please," Chance said before I could even address Sam's jab. I wished Chance would look at me again, but his eyes remained on his menu.

"Make that two," Sam said. "Unless you're feeling off-balance today. Then I'll just have water." A grin spread across Sam's face, making his eyes dance. "Tea leaves a stain."

Anger bubbled in my stomach and embarrassment made my skin heat. "I think I'll be fine," I said, my voice low.

Unfortunately, Sam had witnessed many of my clumsier moments, here in the diner and back in school. In fact, Sam had been at the root of the event that I still relived when I found myself alone in darker moments—it was one of those defining high school turning points that sets in your mind who you are destined to be in this world. I blamed Sam almost completely for the humiliation and self-loathing I'd suffered through for years as a result of that one. And just when I'd almost recovered from that—but hadn't forgiven him by a long shot for the role he'd played, he'd been front and center for a wardrobe malfunction of epic proportions on the stage at senior prom. That last one might not have been his fault, but both events were humiliating, both were tied inextricably to Sam Palmer, and both were things I'd rather never have to think about again.

"If you're having a stable day, then I'll have the iced tea," Sam said. His eyes were still on me, though they looked a little less cheerful than when I'd first walked up. At least he was sensitive enough to know when he'd been rude.

I turned and walked away, slowly and carefully, my mood darker than it had been before. Every time Sam made a sarcastic comment or pointed out one of my deficiencies, I felt small. He knew way too much about me, and I didn't want his jerky antics to color any chances I might have of finally catching his older brother's attention.

"How'd it go?" Maddie whispered when I was back behind the counter.

"Oh great," I said. "They basically asked me not to spill anything on them."

Maddie rolled her eyes. "Sam doesn't mean anything by it. What did Chance say?"

"I think the menu is more interesting than I am." I poured the iced tea and got ready to return to deliver it. Maddie was giving me an evaluative look, her eyes running the length of my body and landing back on my face. "What?" I hissed.

"I have a dress I think will look fantastic on you. Maybe help you catch Chance's attention?"

My jean skirt suddenly made me feel immature and childish. I felt my face heat.

"I don't mean that you don't look great now, Miranda. That isn't what I meant at all." She was backpedaling.

I shook my head. "No, it's okay. I'm not exactly a fashion plate." Denim and flannel were pretty much my go-to uniform when I wasn't changing things up with my maroon polyester diner polo—and Maddie actually was kind of a fashionista. She'd toned down the heels and skinny black pants once she'd realized how impractical they were in the mountains, but she still looked better than most full-time mountain folks I'd ever met.

"Come over tomorrow. You can see if you like the dress?"

I nodded. "Sure. Thanks." A while ago, Maddie had offered to give me some advice about how to catch Chance's attention. I guessed she might know what she was doing, since she had managed to snag Connor Charles last fall—the guy most people couldn't even get to say hello to them. He sat pounding away at his laptop most days while she was working, pausing to smile at her sometimes. He was definitely good-looking, if you liked the norse God look, which let's face it—most women did. He was also ridiculously wealthy and successful. His career as a novelist had taken off years ago and showed no signs of quitting.

"Hey," I ventured. "Still up for giving me some tips, too?" I asked her. "I'm not sure there's much to work with here." I'd looked pretty much the same since graduating high school four years before. Kings Grove wasn't really a fashion mecca. Some of the old timers made fun of Maddie for being on the cutting edge of fashion for this environment. I didn't need inappropriate footwear to be at the butt of jokes, though. I just needed to try to walk across a parking lot without falling down—a nearly impossible feat. I was born with the clumsy gene front and center in my genetic makeup.

She nodded once, her curls falling around her cheeks. "I'll share what little I know." She grinned at me and I turned to deliver iced tea.

"Two iced teas," I said, carefully placing the drinks in front of the Palmer brothers. I coaxed a false brightness into my voice. Thinking about Maddie offering to update my wardrobe and give me tips about how to interact with men only made me suspect I was even more completely hopeless than I'd imagined. No wonder Chance barely noticed I was alive. "What else can I get for you guys?"

Chance had put his menu down and was staring at his phone, but when I asked this question, he turned his eyes to me and I had to take a steadying breath. "A burger sounds great, Miranda. Fries and maybe some coleslaw?"

I nodded, the force of his gaze and his deep voice combining to render me incapable of speech.

"Same here," Sam said, pulling my gaze his way. Where Chance was all suave sophistication—as much as that was possible covered in dust—Sam was just Sam. Sure, he was every bit as searingly sexy as Chance, but didn't matter because it seemed like every time I made a misstep, Sam was there to point it out, and that made me like him a lot less. I was on my guard with Sam—off balance. He was quick with a snarky comment, and honestly, I never could tell what his angle was. I wasn't sure if he really was an asshole, because it really seemed like he was only that way with me, but either way, it put me on edge.

Chance had been three years ahead of us in school. I'd only ever really known him as a distant icon of everything that was masculine. When we were freshmen, Chance was a senior, and he had been ridiculously handsome even then, long before Sam had grown into his looks. But Chance had never looked at me in school. And the one time I thought maybe the heavens had opened and somehow Chance had noticed me, it had turned out to be a cruel joke, which was part of why I couldn't trust Sam, because of the part he'd played in it.

And then Chance had gone away to college. I figured a guy like Chance would never return to Kings Grove. He had way too much going for him. But family is a strong draw, I guess, and when his dad got sick and couldn't run the business, Chance returned to do it. He had a newly minted MBA when he got back.

"I'll go put in your order," I told them, and spun around. I had the distinct feeling Sam's eyes were still on me as I walked away. I glanced back over my shoulder to see, and ran directly into my father, who'd just walked in with Mom.

"Steady there," he chuckled, grabbing me by the shoulders and keeping me on my feet.

"Thanks, Dad," I said, forcing a smile for him as I gathered my senses together post-collision. He'd cleaned up and he smelled like soap and home.

"Any time," he said. "Can you grab us some Cokes?" He and Mom sat down at the long counter and I went to put in the Palmers' order, hoping that they hadn't been watching when I'd run right into Dad.

The place was packed, so I didn't have much time to chat with my parents, and it took all of my focus to get from one place to another without incident. When the food was up for the Palmers, I checked to be sure my path was clear before loading up with plates. Once they were successfully delivered, I let myself relax a bit as I stood next to their table.

"You planning to stay up here, Miranda?" Chance's eyes were on my face.

Oh God, he was gorgeous.

My brain stopped working and words refused to come as the blood rushed into my face. His hair was a light brown, perfectly tousled, and he had a quarter-inch scruff over his jaw that made me want to run my fingers over it. Or maybe my tongue. His teeth were straight and white, and his broad chest was challenging the plaid work shirt he wore as his muscles bulged beneath it.

Say something. "I ... I don't know," I managed. *Brilliant.*

"Well," Chance put a fry in his mouth and tilted his head, looking thoughtful. "You're way too smart to waitress for the rest of your life."

I nodded, then stopped myself. Agreeing with him was arrogant. I tried to keep my head still and look like I was listening and not hanging on every delicious word from his lips. His very full, perfectly proportioned lips.

"We're looking to hire an admin assistant," Chance continued. "Part time. Nothing big, but we need kind of a problem solver."

"We need someone to answer the phone," Sam said, his voice flat.

I swung my gaze to Sam and narrowed my eyes at him.

"She doesn't want to do that," Sam finished, looking at his brother.

"I can totally do that." The words were out before my brain had engaged. For as long as I could remember I'd conditioned myself to say 'yes' to Chance Palmer, and to hold my own with his brother if I felt like he was putting me down in some way. It turned out not to matter what Chance was asking.

Chance smiled and shook his head. "No, I meant, I thought you might know someone ... your age?"

My face undoubtedly fell as my heart sank. *My age?* He saw me as a kid.

"Uh, hello? She's *my* age," Sam said to his brother. "Don't make it sound like it's a disease just 'cuz you're getting all old and withered." So it turned out Sam's attitude wasn't reserved only for me. That was good to know, at least.

Still, this was not going well at all. And what the hell was Sam doing jumping to my defense? It was confusing.

"I can't think of anyone off the top of my head," I said. "I'll keep my eyes open though."

Chance wasn't asking me after all. He was hoping for someone else. I didn't know if I should take that as a compliment or an insult.

"Thanks Miranda," Chance said, putting another fry in his mouth. He was always so calm, so confident. I envied him as much as I wanted him. He'd go on about his day, having no idea that this simple conversation would have me stressing out and rethinking every word I'd uttered for weeks. I was hopeless.

Chapter 4

SAM

Shit.

Seriously. *Shit.*

Any time Miranda George got near me my brain turned to complete mush. But not the kind of mush that made people stupid or dumb—where they just became charmingly inarticulate. That would have been greatly preferable. Instead, my brain defaulted to asshole. Maybe that was my basic nature. When Miranda got near me with her cute little curvy body, her swinging blond ponytail and infectious smile, I turned into a complete asshole.

Because if I didn't?

Well, if I wasn't an asshole to her I might just end up confessing that I'd been in love with her since I was five.

And we couldn't have that.

So when she walked away from our booth, thinking I was a dick for saying she'd get through school faster if she didn't work at a diner, it was probably for the best. Because what I'd wanted to say was something closer to, "Why would you want to get a degree that might enable you to leave Kings Grove ... and me?"

Kings Grove wasn't exactly a big town. Hell, it was barely a town. And imagining life here without Miranda…

Well, I couldn't imagine it.

So why the hell did I keep pushing her away?

Mostly because she pushed me first.

Chapter 5

MIRANDA

"You're not hopeless," Maddie said, circling me as I perched on a barstool at Connor's house.

"Far from hopeless," Connor agreed, sipping a beer and nodding, the kitchen lights catching his red-gold hair as he stood behind the counter.

"Connor," Maddie said, turning toward him. "I love you, but you're probably not needed here right now." She must've picked up on the way I flinched when Connor chimed in. Maybe "not hopeless" was intended to be a compliment, but any man's opinion was hard to take objectively.

"I see how it is." Connor pretended to be offended and came around the counter to give Maddie a kiss. "I'll just take the laptop up to my bedroom. I'm writing a scene where I need to kill off a curly-haired crazy woman, anyway."

"We both know I never die in your books," Maddie said, raising an eyebrow at him. There was a Maddie character in every one of his books, and had been even before they'd met again as adults. It was part of what brought them together—the romantic mysterious coincidence of it all.

I watched Connor ascend the stairs and shook my head. "I want that."

"Sorry. That's mine," she said.

"No!" I felt myself blushing. "I mean, I want what you guys have. You're so happy, so comfortable."

"Well it wasn't always that way," she said.

I remembered well the struggles they'd faced to be together. Between ex-husbands and the police, it was a small miracle they'd made it through. "I know."

"And I kissed a lot of frogs first," she said. "But hopefully you won't have to."

I ducked my chin and looked up at her, the dark rim of my glasses providing a shelter I'd grown used to. Behind the lenses I felt protected and safe.

"First," Maddie said. "What do you say we lose the frames?"

I shook my head. "I'm clumsy enough when I can see. Blind? I'd be screwed."

"Contacts?"

"I do have some. But they're not super comfortable. Especially when the air is really dry."

"Like always."

"Especially lately." The newscast in the background was predicting more of the same. Namely, no rain for California.

"Well, glasses are pretty retro, and these are really cute as glasses go, so forget I said anything there. To be honest, I don't think there's much about your looks that needs any kind of fixing."

"So it's just my personality?" I said, slumping.

"No!" Maddie looked stricken. "I didn't mean that at all! Miranda, this isn't about fixing anything that's broken. Because nothing is! There is nothing at all wrong with you exactly the way you are. You know that, right?"

I looked up, meeting her eye. I wasn't exactly insecure, but even a confident independent girl had things she wouldn't mind changing. Especially if those things prevented the man of her dreams from seeing her as a potential match for him.

"You are smart and funny, genuine and sweet. You're gorgeous..." She stood up and took a step away, shaking her head as I started to protest. "And you're pretty tough, too, I think."

"Why do you think I'm tough?"

"This isn't an easy place to live your whole life," she said. "Harsh winters, not a lot of luxuries ... and the kind of close community where everyone knows everyone else's business. And ..." she paused, eyeing me sideways as if she thought I might jump at her, "anyone who has as many little accidents as you do has developed a thick skin and the ability to laugh at herself."

I nodded. I definitely had that. I had no choice. If I couldn't laugh at myself, I'd end up crying most days.

"So I'm not trying to change you, and I wouldn't let anyone else ever tell you to change, either."

"I thought that's what this was about?"

"No. This is about taking the things that are already amazing and bringing them forward so silly men with no observational powers might pay more attention to what's right in front of them."

"That sounds good."

Maddie gave me a focused look. "Maybe a stronger eyeliner?"

"I can do that." Maybe this would be easier than I thought.

"And no more denim skirts."

I had like twelve denim skirts. I lived in denim skirts. "Um ..."

"I mean, they're cute, it's just ... they're cute. Like high-school cute."

"Point taken." I hadn't upgraded my wardrobe in years. Evidently it showed.

"I think you need to shake things up a bit. Make Chance see you as the woman you are. You said he's known you since you were a kid?"

I nodded.

"Then he needs to be reminded that you're not a kid anymore."

"I can't exactly wear cocktail dresses to work."

"Well, not to the diner."

"Maddie!" I stood up. This was not going to work. "I'm just not a cocktail dress kind of girl! Woman. Whatever."

She put her hands on my shoulders and sat me back down. "I know that." Her face softened.

I relaxed a little bit. Maddie had been a good friend, and she'd been through plenty of tough times herself. Even if she couldn't help me here, I trusted her enough to listen.

"Okay. Fashion show time. Want a drink?" Maddie went to the refrigerator and pulled out two beers, handing me one after she'd opened it.

I didn't usually drink, but I didn't want to hurt her feelings, so I took the beer and wandered the room a bit, looking around. There was an incredible stone fireplace that dominated one side of the room. It was actually carved into a huge boulder that the house had been built around, and it was stunning as the fire inside the rock glowed and danced. The other side of the room was all glass panes, looking out over a deck outside and a verdant meadow just past the deck. Sadly, with the lack of water in the past couple years, the edges of the meadow were brown and wilted. "I bet this was incredible when the water was here," I said.

Maddie nodded. "I haven't seen it like that, but I bet you're right. Everything up here brightens when there's enough water." We looked out the window for a minute and then

Maddie turned to me again. "Okay, so can I give you a few things?"

Maddie disappeared upstairs and came back down with an armful of clothes, which she dumped onto the couch. "A lot of this stuff doesn't fit me anymore. I've rounded out a bit since meeting Connor. He keeps feeding me." She grinned and waved me toward the clothes.

"I can't," I said. Maddie's stuff was super high end. She'd been the society type, living in big cities before she moved up here.

"Of course you can." Maddie pulled out a blue shirtdress with a tied belt that was adorable. And designer. "This would look great on you! Kind of an upgrade from the denim skirt, but still casual and comfortable. Will you try it on?"

I raised an eyebrow at her. I didn't like charity—and I didn't need it. But her clothes were adorable. And much nicer than anything I'd ever choose for myself, and this felt more like girlfriends having a fashion show than like charity. "I'll try it on," I said. "But you can't give all this stuff to me. My mother will freak out."

"Your mom?"

"She'll take it as another sign that her failing business is making people around here feel sorry for her and give us stuff."

Maddie laughed. "That's kind of dramatic."

"You have met my mom, right?"

"I guess she is a little dramatic. She was a godsend when I moved in here, though. Once I got all my stuff back from Jack's, she helped me find ways to fit it all in without making Connor feel like he had to move out."

"She did mention you had a lot of stuff."

"So she'll understand why I'm downsizing!" Maddie pushed the dress into my hands, turning me toward the bathroom beneath the staircase.

In the bathroom I pulled off my skirt and stepped into the

dress, cinching the belt around my waist. It was comfortable, that was true. I turned to face the full-length mirror on the back of the door. The dress was cute. I just wasn't sure it looked right on me. I definitely looked different. I lingered in front of the mirror for a moment, gazing at myself. I didn't generally care what I looked like, and I hadn't spent a lot of time worrying about it before. Maddie was right, though—a heavier eyeliner would make my blue eyes pop behind the dark frames of my glasses. And I could probably stand to brighten my lips a bit. The blond ponytail that had become my everyday style was probably not doing me any favors, either. I pulled the elastic from my hair and let it fall down around my face, covering my shoulders and brushing the top of my chest. It had a natural wave, and when I ran my fingers through it a bit, it didn't look half bad. Maybe I could upgrade my look a bit. It wouldn't be that difficult.

I stepped out of the bathroom and nearly ran right into Connor as he walked by. That was the kind of timing I'd always been blessed with.

"Woah!" He cried, stepping back. Then he stopped moving and literally stared at me. "Woah," he said again, his voice softer. "Miranda ... you look fantastic." There was a glimmer of something in his eyes that I had only seen in movies and on television—the glimmer that appears when a man is looking at a woman he finds attractive. It wasn't predatory, or threatening. But it was heady. *Did I do that?*

"Holy ..." Maddie stepped to Connor's side.

I don't know where I found the nerve, but I did a little spin for them.

"You have to keep that dress," Maddie said. "And you should definitely wear your hair down sometimes. Miranda, you're gorgeous!"

A smile took over my face. I felt gorgeous as they looked at me. I'd never felt ugly, but I'd never really bothered to try doing anything to enhance my appearance. "I wonder if Chance would even notice," I said.

"He'll notice," Connor said, then turned and got a bottle of water from the refrigerator. "Drink?"

"No thanks." I walked back over to the window and eyed the beer I'd left sitting there. Drinking had never been my thing. I hadn't had a drink since high school, and that had gone particularly badly. It turns out that mixing me with alcohol—especially in a backyard with a swimming pool—just ends up with me becoming very, very wet. I didn't think now was a good time to try again.

"Connor," Maddie said, her voice full of mock-scolding. "Aren't you supposed to be upstairs writing?"

Connor grinned sheepishly. "I've tried to explain to you that the reason it takes a while to write a book is because writers spend half their time looking for reasons not to write." He shrugged.

Maddie shook her head and turned back to me.

"I'm not sure it really matters what I look like, though," I said, picking up where my brain had left me. "As soon as I move, I'll inevitably fall or trip or drop something scalding into his lap …" All of these things had happened to me, and worse.

"Well, there isn't much we can do about that," Maddie said, looking thoughtful. "But if you want the truth, all of that is kind of adorable. I mean, maybe not the scalding soup in the lap thing. That wasn't so good." Maddie had been there when that one had happened. I'd followed it up by dumping a glass of ice water into the same spot, in hopes of saving Chance's family jewels. He'd looked at me like I'd lost my mind. The thought of hurting him—of hurting him there, especially—was almost more than I could stomach, and the memory made my eyes water. It had been a very bad day. I could still hear Sam cracking up as he'd watched the whole thing go down.

"Will you try on a few of these other things?" Maddie was

holding up a soft shirt with flowers on it. It would go great with a denim skirt, I thought. But then she handed me a pair of khaki capris. "These work together," she said. She made a few more outfits out of the mountain on the couch, and Connor watched with a smile on his face.

"Okay, so once he notices I look different, what then?" I sat down next to the mountain.

"Then you charm him," Maddie said.

"By not spilling things." I said, skeptical.

"That's a start, but how about asking about him? Do you know what kind of things he does in his spare time? Sports, hobbies?"

Wracking my mind, I came up with nothing. "Not really."

"He doesn't have much family, so that's probably not a great topic," Maddie said, chewing her lip as she thought. "What about work? You can always ask him about work."

She had a point. "Actually, he mentioned that they're looking for an administrative person. Someone to answer phones and stuff. He asked if I knew anyone."

Maddie clapped her hands together in excitement. "You totally know someone!"

"You?" My heart sank. Why would Maddie want to do that? She already had her photography business and the diner. And Connor.

"No, not me. You."

I nodded. I had wanted Chance to ask me if I was interested in the position when he'd brought it up. "I thought of that."

"So volunteer yourself. I mean, to be paid, of course."

"Right."

"And then you'll be around him a lot more often. He won't have a chance once he realizes how sweet and smart and incredible you are. He just needs to see you in a new light, away from the diner. A new, more professional job is perfect."

"Even if he's my boss?"

Maddie tilted her head to the side, thinking. "I don't think that's a big deal. That's how small businesses work—friends and family all pitching in."

I wondered if I could stomach working with Sam. I didn't mind seeing him at the diner, but having to take direction from him might be too much. Maybe I could give it a try if it meant more time with Chance, though. I'd just ignore his brother. "I'll ask them about it again."

"Great! We have a plan! And a wardrobe. What could go wrong?" Maddie said.

I stood, scooping the clothes into my arms. The sleeve of one of the shirts caught the top of my full beer bottle and pulled it off the table, sending the bottle crashing to the floor below, spewing bubbling suds everywhere. "Right. What could go wrong?" I leaned over to pick up the bottle, but Connor was already there.

"I got it," he said. "No worries."

I smiled and hugged Maddie goodbye. "Sorry about the rug, Connor."

"It's a cabin," he said, smiling. "Nothing fancy to ruin here." Every expensive piece of furniture around us begged loudly to differ, but I appreciated his nonchalance. "See you guys later."

I made my way out to my car with caution, dropping the clothes into the back seat and thanking my stars that my bad luck hadn't extended to my driving skills.

Chapter 6
MIRANDA

The Palmer Construction offices were situated just down the main highway from Kings Grove's small downtown center. And by center, people really meant 'parking lot.' The whole of Kings Grove—the diner, the post office, the lodge, the ranger station and visitor center, the hardware store, and the small grocery store—all faced a central parking lot with a road leading in on both sides. One of the entrances came in from the main highway—that's the direction from which visitors usually arrived. The other road led back toward the village, which was about two miles away, and was where most of the residents lived. There were cabins scattered here and there, but most were clustered around a central meadow in the village proper. A few scattered offices and convenience stores were set just outside the downtown parking lot along the main highway, and Palmer Construction was one of these.

Chance and Sam shared the business, which they had assumed when their father passed away. Sam had always worked for his dad, though he'd gone to college part-time down in Fresno, too. Chance had never intended to remain in

Kings Grove—or at least it didn't seem so. He'd graduated high school and been the talk of the town when he accepted admission to U.C. Berkeley and then went on to get his MBA at Stanford. The locals had celebrated his success, and were both saddened and pleased when Kings Grove's big success story returned to the fold to take over for his dad.

My pick-up truck fit nicely in the small lot just in front of the office, next to the huge Palmer Construction truck and near the collection of backhoes and tractors the men used for their business. The beat-up blue truck I called my own already looked at home. Chance's car was here too, a giant black SUV that walked the line between a work truck and a luxury vehicle, and I tried to push down the nerves bundling in my stomach at the thought of talking to him.

The solid wood door swung out easily when I pulled, and my heart began beating a quicker rhythm as Chance's distinctive low voice rolled out the open door of an office adjacent to the lobby.

"If it gets any worse, let me know, John. We'll lend a hand." I could see Chance's back as he stood looking out the window behind his desk, the phone to his ear.

"Miranda. What's up?" There was an office on each side of the small reception space, and Sam appeared from the side opposite Chance's office, no doubt summoned by the bell above the front door.

"Hey Sam." My eyes were locked on Chance's broad back, a dark flannel pulled tightly across the muscles just below the curls that were beginning to form at the top of his tanned neck. I pulled my gaze away to land on Sam instead. His familiar face was hardly a comfort. Chance and Sam's eyes were almost identical, and the angular cut of their cheekbones and jaws were similar too. Both Palmer brothers could have been carved from stone—they were that good looking.

Despite their similar faces, I swooned when Chance looked

at me, and I definitely felt something when my eyes met Sam's —only I wasn't sure exactly what it was. He made me nervous. Not in a good way, but in a way that kept me on my toes. And the way he was staring at me now made me uncomfortable. Like he was trying to figure something out. I was suddenly regretting wearing my hair down.

Best get to the point. "I came in to ask about that job. The administrative one?" My fingers found the tassel on my purse and began pulling at it.

Sam stepped out of his office and squinted at me as one side of his mouth lifted in a half-smile. He looked confused, his face crinkling up. "Why?"

Annoyance flooded me. This was the problem with Sam. Nothing was straightforward. I sighed, turning to see if Chance might be done with his call and come out so I could speak to him instead. Of course then I'd be nervous instead of annoyed. "I thought I might be able to help out with that."

"It's not a 'help out' type of thing. It's a job. And you already have a job. And you're in school." Sam leaned his tall body against the door jam of his office and crossed his big arms over his broad chest. He gave off an air of judgment that put me on edge. And of course he was being difficult about something that could be simple.

"But Chance said it was part time?"

"What part of the time do you see yourself being here?" He was smiling now and I got the distinct impression he was toying with me. I shifted my weight uncomfortably as I stood there, in Maddie's khaki pants and flowered blouse. The clothes had me feeling a bit unlike myself, and now I was standing here like an idiot in the middle of the room and Sam was being difficult. I had no doubt Chance would have offered me a seat. He was the polite brother. Sam was just watching me, like I was put there to amuse him.

"The part of the time when you guys need me, I guess."

My voice didn't carry the confident edge I wanted it to, so I cleared my throat and continued. "I can rearrange my diner shifts if I need to, and college is online. I do most of my work at night anyway."

"Right." Sam chewed on his bottom lip for a second and then something about his fingernails caught his attention. He brought his hand to his face and rubbed his thumb against his index finger, looking intently at it. Finally he tucked his hand back under the opposite elbow and looked back up at me. "Okay." He stood upright again and turned around to head back into his office, leaving me standing in the middle of the room.

Okay? What did that mean?

"Hey Miranda," Chance appeared in the other doorway, having finished his call. My head snapped around as Chance called my name. "Wow," he said, "you look really nice today."

Maybe Maddie had been right about the denim skirts.

"Thanks." I couldn't help shaking my head to let my blond curls dance a bit around my shoulders. Chance looked nice too, but I wasn't about to mention it. His defined cheekbones and dark eyebrows gave him a serious look, and the vague stubble along his chin was the sexiest thing I could imagine. In fact, I did imagine it. A lot. How it would be a little bit rough, but also soft, and how it would rub my chin when he kissed me.

"Can I help you with something?" Chance asked, smiling to reveal those perfect white teeth. He was definitely too good looking for Kings Grove.

My blood was rushing, but I forced myself to remain in one spot—less chance of knocking things over if I didn't move. As words formed on my lips, Sam's voice came from his office.

"Just hired her."

Chance's eyebrows shot up and the eyes found my face as he moved in to tidy up the desk in front of me. "Hired you?"

"The admin position," Sam called, still not coming back into the room. *Rude.*

Chance stuck his head into his brother's office. "You did? We didn't even talk about it."

Oh God, Chance didn't want me to work here. I was going to be hired and fired in a five-minute span.

Of course I was. That was perfect.

"Didn't need to. She's way smarter than we need and she's flexible. Miranda's on top of stuff, Chance. She'll be great." Sam's voice had said these words, but I was having a hard time believing it. I was used to Sam laughing at me or making fun of me when I did something clumsy, I was not used to him expressing confidence in me. Not at all.

Chance turned back around and gave me an appraising look, taking in everything with his shrewd cool eyes, his head cocked slightly to the side. "Sounds good to me, then," he said finally. "When can you start?"

"Um ..." That wasn't a question I'd actually considered in my concern about just coming in and talking to them. "Now?"

A wide smile lit Chance's face and it nearly toppled me with its beauty. "How about tomorrow? Let me get some stuff ready to show you, okay?"

"Yeah, that would be ..." My words were stunted by Chance's proximity and presence. How did he manage to so completely fill every room he was in? "That would be perfect." My smile was much too big for someone accepting a job offer, but it felt perma-fixed on my face. "We'll talk about salary and everything then?" At least I'd remembered to ask one of the important questions.

"We can talk about it now," Chance said. "We'll pay you fifteen bucks an hour. Does that sound fair?"

That was more than fair. I didn't make that at the diner, that was for sure. "Great," I said, trying not to sound too excited.

"Good then," Chance said. "See you tomorrow? Noon?"

That was perfect, since I had a breakfast shift at the diner.

"We can work out the rest of the week's schedule then," Chance said. "Bring your schedule from the diner."

"Okay," I said. "Thanks." My heart fluttered an excited beat and I turned to go out, essentially crashing through the front door before finding myself in the parking lot. I was going to be that close to Chance every day. How on earth would I handle it?

I crossed back to my truck, lifting my face to the wind blowing in from the canyons beyond. There was something different in the air. I couldn't put my finger on it, but it set me on edge, reminding me of my grandmother's wacky pronouncements about "earthquake weather." I didn't want to think about whatever it might be—probably nothing. So I hopped into the truck and headed back toward home, thoughts of Chance's gleaming smile heavy on my mind.

Chapter 7

SAM

This was not ideal.

Miranda was going to be working here?

I'd practically kicked my brother when he'd mentioned it to her at the diner, and had been relieved when they'd both let it drop.

It wasn't that I didn't want to be around Miranda. It was actually the complete opposite of that.

Miranda George had an effect on me. It was something I'd never really experienced with anyone else, and that alone made me worry, but mostly I just hated myself around her. She made me self-conscious and I found myself worrying about ridiculous things in her presence, like why my feet suddenly seemed so huge, and whether my hair was a disaster. Generally speaking, I was a confident guy—as confident as any guy can be when he spends his life in his charming big brother's shadow. But around Miranda? I wasn't confident. I was something else.

Like I said, I was an asshole.

If anyone had called me on it, I wouldn't have been able to explain it clearly. It was something about the way she made me feel—giddy and happy, and painfully nervous at the same time.

Throw in her completely obvious crush on my brother, and my body kicked up some kind of chemical reaction that bubbled into asshole mode. And everything out of my mouth around her was pretty much awful.

I wished there was some way I could just have a real shot with her.

Miranda had a big heart and an openness to the world that had always charmed me completely, even when we'd been in first grade together and she'd kicked a fourth-grade friend of Chance's who was teasing me. Maybe that was what had sealed my affection for her. Back then, when she'd been this tiny and fierce little blonde dynamo, we'd been friends.

But once we'd gotten into middle school and I'd begun to realize how I felt about her, things had gotten awkward. And her admiration for my brother had become clear. But she'd still come over to my house sometimes after school, and her parents would invite my dad over for dinner, so we'd tag along.

But then the THING had happened freshman year in high school and all hope had pretty much been lost.

It had been Chance's senior year, his send-off party for Berkeley. Chance had never planned to stay in Kings Grove. He'd gotten into a good school, and we were all gathered to celebrate the end of the school year, and to say goodbye. (Some of us more gleefully than others.)

Miranda and I were freshmen, but since I lived in the house where the party was taking place, I was there. And so were some other freshmen I'd invited, including Miranda. And I regretted those invitations now like I'd never regretted anything before or since. I was the reason she'd been there. And at the time, she'd thought she was lucky to be invited to a senior party.

But then Sophie Weiland had decided to be cruel. To both of us.

I don't know how Sophie knew about Miranda's crush on

my brother—though I guess most of the school just knew these things. It wasn't like we were at a school of five hundred kids, after all. Kings Grove is tiny. So we kind of knew each other's business. And Sophie wasn't a nice girl at the best of times. But when she had potentially sensitive information? She was downright diabolical.

And her actions led Miranda to believe she had a shot with my brother—and led me to think I might have a chance with Miranda.

But neither of those things was true. We'd both been Sophie's pawns when she'd whispered into our ears that night. And when Miranda figured out that Chance hadn't actually invited her to meet him out in the woodshed to say a quiet goodbye and tell her something he'd always wanted to say; when she'd found me waiting there instead because Sophie said *she'd* invited *me*; when she'd bolted outside to find a crowd of seniors standing around and laughing hysterically—she assumed I'd been in on it. And I'd never really gotten the opportunity to tell her I'd been played every bit as much as she had. Because that would have meant admitting why I'd been in that shed.

I'd never forget how she'd turned back to look at me standing inside the darkened space as everyone outside laughed at us. But she thought they were only laughing at her. Her eyes had filled with angry tears, and she'd said, "I hate you, Sam."

So yeah. That was bad.

But our shared history actually gets worse.

We kind of went our separate ways after freshman year—as much as that is possible at a school of only 150 kids. And we made it to senior prom, though I still had a fierce crush on Miranda and had begun to say horrible things to her instead of admitting that all I wanted was to sit quietly next to her and hold her hand. Maybe do some other things my teenaged body hadn't tried yet but my mind had been busily working on for years.

Somehow, we'd both been elected to prom court—Miranda because she was gorgeous and sweet to absolutely everyone, and me because…well, who knows why, really? And that isn't the point. The point is that there was a moment when we both had to get up on the stage at the front of the dance floor under the glittering lights reflecting around the room, with the swell of music surrounding us, and the cheers of our classmates in our ears. And unfortunately, Miranda has a tiny bit of trouble in high-pressure situations—not to mention high heels—so she tripped over the hem of her long spaghetti-strap dress on the way up the stairs at the side of the stage, and went crashing to the floor in front of the crowd.

And you'd probably figure that was the worst of it. But you'd be wrong.

So wrong.

Miranda was pretty accustomed to falling down, and so she popped right back up unhurt, though she gave me a dirty look and whispered, "Thanks a lot," as I ascended the stairs behind her.

I didn't think I'd tripped her. Maybe I had. The whole memory feels like it's penned in permanent marker in my mind, but maybe the edges are a little fuzzy now.

The nerves must've been racing through her—I know I was nervous. Too nervous to give her a good once over like I should have, to make sure she was all put back together before we were officially presented to the school. And so I didn't notice it right away.

Not until the crowd in front of the stage began to come alive with a faint titter that morphed quickly into a roar of laughter. The kids in front of the stage pointed up at where Miranda's dress was tugged down way too low in front.

And I didn't act fast enough. I should have figured it out right away. I should have stepped in front of her, protected her.

But I was seventeen. And part of me thought they might be laughing at me, and seventeen-year old boys are not known for their self-confidence or their chivalry.

It just took me too long to figure it out.

Miranda had stared out at the crowd, her dress pulled down much lower than it should have been, and more of her assets on parade than she ever would have intended, and it took her a while to figure it out too. And then we both saw it at the same time. She yelped and crossed her arms in front of her chest, and I finally did step in front of her, facing her and putting my arms around her to try to shield her from eyes that didn't deserve to see any more of her than she wanted to show.

"Get off me, Sam!" She hissed, tears running down her face as she struggled in my arms.

All I could think was that I wanted to cover her. I wanted to protect her. I wanted to hold her tight and keep her safe where no one could ever hurt her.

And all she wanted was to get off that stage as quickly as possible. And I was holding her there.

Chance had been standing off to one side, home on spring break and humiliatingly acting as a chaperone. And when he saw what was going on, it took him all of a second to remove his tux jacket, stride to Miranda, and tuck it around her, pushing me off of her in the process.

"Smooth move, bro," he'd whispered to me as he turned her to the stairs, his arm protectively over her shoulders as he guided her out of the spotlight.

He was her white knight. As usual.

And I was the guy she hated.

Chapter 8
MIRANDA

I arrived for my early shift at the restaurant the next day with something like excitement brewing in my heart. I'd been doing the same thing—studying, living at home, working at the diner—for so long I'd forgotten there might be other options, and that those other options could be really good for me. Even without Chance's presence at Palmer Construction, the idea of a new challenge was welcome. The stormy gray-blue eyes and chiseled jaw in the next office over wouldn't hurt either. And I definitely didn't mean Sam's.

"Someone's awfully cheerful today." Adele frowned at me as I tied on my apron behind the counter. Only someone as terminally un-cheerful as Adele would look annoyed when one of her employees showed up happy for a five-thirty AM shift.

"I guess I am," I said. The air outside had been warm this morning, as it always was in summer. The dry warmth of the mountains and the cool moisture misting up off the meadow in the center of the village always made the mornings seem ethereal, like fairies might be flitting around, playing on the light breeze. No fairies had popped out as I'd driven by the big grassy expanse this morning, but two deer had lifted their heads up out of the fog to watch me roll by.

"Glad to see it, Miranda." Adele's husband, Frank, was the cheery one between them. His head appeared through the window behind the counter and he grinned at me.

The regulars began to appear in ones and twos, rangers who went out early for work inside the Park and professional folks who drove down to the valley every day for office jobs. The morning swirled by, filled with pancakes and eggs, coffee and tea. The sun rose beyond the building housing the diner and the bright rays poured into the parking lot outside, coloring the world in hues of yellow and orange. In the time before Maddie arrived at nine, I'd spilled on only one customer and managed not to trip at all. So far, it was an amazing morning.

Maddie was not a morning person. She needed at least two cups of coffee before she could hold an actual conversation. But I was bursting with the need to tell her about the new job. I watched while she tied her burgundy apron around her waist and gathered her hair into a wild knot at the back of her head, trying to see if she looked more awake than usual.

"You're making me nervous," she said as she washed her hands, looking at me sideways.

"Sorry," I said. "Just excited today."

"Need coffee," she replied.

I pulled a mug from the counter and poured her a cup, setting it behind her on the counter. She turned around and doctored it with cream and sugar, and then lifted the cup to her lips.

"Most places expect employees to show up awake," Adele quipped from the podium by the door.

"I'm awake," Maddie said. "Just finishing up the caffeination process."

They both knew she could probably do without the waitressing gig, so I doubted Adele would push too hard. They'd never really gotten along, but there was some kind of grudging respect between them. And Frank would never let Adele actually fire Maddie.

Maddie pulled a bag of sugar packets from below the counter and set to work filling the little silver tins along the countertop. "Okay, so why are you dancing around and grinning like that?"

"I start my new job at noon."

Maddie's hand stopped, still buried in the big bag of sugar packs. Her eyes widened. "You're leaving the diner?"

I shook my head. "Doing both. Starting at Palmer Construction part time today."

She grinned. "You did it. That's wonderful, Miranda!" Her voice was low enough that Adele couldn't hear, for which I was glad. She wouldn't like it, and I didn't intend to ask her opinion. "And that dress looks amazing on you."

I was wearing the shirt-dress I'd modeled at Maddie and Connor's place. "Thanks." A warm blush crawled up my cheeks.

"I can't wait to hear all about it," she said, nodding at a customer who'd just taken a seat at the end of the counter.

The breakfast shift kept us busy until about eleven, when the usual pre-lunch lull hit, and we worked to tidy things up for the next wave. Another server, Dean Apcott, had been hired when he'd come back home this spring, and he arrived just as we were finishing up.

Dean was a local kid who was supposed to be away at college, but who had taken a year off. He'd been the most recent hope for something big to come out of Kings Grove High—a soccer star and science and math prodigy. But something had gone wrong in his first year at school, because he'd been back before the year was up. His parents were tight-lipped about it, and Dean would only say that he'd needed a break.

"What up, ladies?" Dean grinned at us as he tucked a pencil behind his ear, his overgrown hair curling in brown locks around it.

"Not much," I told him. "How's it going?"

"Can't complain," he said. He leaned forward, resting his weight on his forearms as he gazed out over the restaurant and out the window. "You guys hear about that fire?"

He had our attention now. "Fire?" Maddie asked.

"Yeah. Probably not a big deal, just a lightening strike on a back ridge a couple days ago. Dad says it'll stay back there and burn itself out." Dean nodded at a table of four that had just been seated for lunch. "Don't freak out," he said, looking over his shoulder as he moved around to take their order.

Maddie and I exchanged a worried glance, but I knew Dean was probably right. Wildfire was a part of being in the mountains. The huge Sequoias around us, the trees that gave Kings Grove its name, needed fire to survive. It had been part of their lives for millennia. But it wasn't so good for humans. And houses. I sent up a silent prayer that the fire would stay in the backcountry. As I made my way out to the truck I took a few extra sniffs of the clear mountain air I loved. There was no trace of smoke, only the verdant scent of lush meadow grass and the spicy combination of pine and redwood.

I pulled up outside Palmer Construction and put on a fresh coat of lip gloss.

Everything was about to change.

Flipping down the mirror in the truck, I took a couple minutes to give myself a little pep talk and to try to squash the nerves that sweep around inside my body whenever the thought of seeing Chance Palmer comes up.

"You can do this." Talking to myself might not be the most

sane thing, but crashing through the door and falling on my face out of sheer nervousness would be so much worse. "You got this." I sat in the car a second longer and nodded, letting the nerves dissipate a bit before getting the creepy feeling someone was watching me. I snapped the mirror shut and whipped my head around, looking for the source of my sixth sense. I didn't have to look far. Sam Palmer stood directly next to my window, grinning at me.

"You talking to yourself now, Miranda?" he asked as I opened the door and got out.

"No," I barked, smoothing my dress as I shut the door behind me.

Sam laughed, a low rolling sound that managed to prick every cell in my body with annoyance. "I find it's easiest to get work done if we go inside."

I let Sam hold the door open for me, even though I had hoped he might be somehow absent during my first day at his office. Sam and his broody presence were no part of the fantasies I had about how my job at Palmer might work out.

As soon as we were inside, I looked around for Chance, my stomach tight with anticipation. But the office off the lobby was quiet, the big chair empty.

"Chance is on a job down in the valley today," Sam said. "So you get me." He said it like he knew I'd be disappointed, his head cocked to one side and a smirk on his face.

"Oh." I couldn't help the flat note of disappointment that fell from my lips.

"Don't sound so excited," Sam said, his tone matching my own. "Your favorite Palmer brother will be back tomorrow."

I tried for a smile, but there was really no point. Sam just rubbed me the wrong way and we both knew it. "Where shall I put my things?" Best to stick to business.

"This is your desk, so wherever you can find space. I cleared out a couple drawers at the bottom here." Sam came around and pulled the chair out for me, opening two big drawers at the bottom of the desk. "This one up here," he pointed to a long top drawer. "It's got all your emergency office supplies."

I nodded, expecting to see pens, Post-Its, and tape stuffing the space when he pulled it open. Instead, the flat drawer rolled open to reveal chapstick, gum, a deck of cards, and three boxes of Raisinets—my favorite. "These are office supplies?"

A little smile pulled at the corner of Sam's face, the golden stubble mixed into his beard glinting in the light. He didn't look up to meet my eye, but kept his gaze focused on the surprising drawer. "I just wanted you to feel at home," he said. He turned and pointed to a cabinet hugging the wall next to the front door. "If you need pens and stuff, they're in the cabinet over there."

"Thanks," I said. I was usually somewhat off balance, but having Sam do something thoughtful had me completely off kilter. What was I supposed to make of this? "Um …okay. So where do we start?"

Sam looked up, the playful smile gone. Time for business. "Have a seat."

I sat and he pulled up a chair next to me, scooting near to pull the mouse into his hand on my right side. He leaned close to reach the keyboard in front of me and I had a strange sudden impression of his size as I leaned back to let his muscled arm stretch across my space. The corded muscles in his forearm flexed, and something warmed inside me in a very unfamiliar way—at least unfamiliar when associated with Sam. I knew other girls found him attractive, but it was almost as if I'd never really seen him before. At least not in the last several years.

Now that he was right in my face and literally in my space, my body seemed to want me to acknowledge the broad muscled back, the big capable hands on the keyboard, the thighs challenging the fabric of his jeans.

"I set up a user account for you. You'll have to change the password when you have time. For now, it's just 'PConstruction1945.' The year my grandfather started this business."

I nodded and watched Sam log into my account, taking a deep breath to force myself to focus. This was Sam, I reminded myself, and it wasn't too hard to will my general dislike for him to overtake whatever strange impulse I'd felt for a moment to thread my fingers through the dark hair at the nape of his neck.

This was Sam, and I was at work. The only finger/hair threading that would be happening would be with Chance. Maybe. Probably not. But that was the idea.

Focus, Miranda.

"So for now, everything you need is on the desktop here." Sam was still leaning over in his chair, his shoulder dangerously close to actually touching mine. The space between our bodies felt charged, like the air was snapping with electric knowledge that if he actually touched me I'd probably jump a mile high and unload every angry comment I'd ever held in where Sam Palmer was concerned. Or maybe something completely different would happen—something worse. I had a vague flash of me kissing him, and then cringed at the thought.

What was wrong with me? The anticipation in the air made me uncomfortable and I scooted away a bit. Sam paused in his description of every single file on my computer and glanced at me with eyes that looked almost hurt.

"Sorry, I was just, uh, stretching." Why was I apologizing for wanting to maintain my personal space?

He nodded, but his look became guarded and he straightened up a bit, moving away from me. "Okay, well, start here with this spreadsheet," he said. A vague scent of some kind of soap moved around him, along with something else I just realized I'd been noticing for a while.

"Why do you smell like licorice?" It was out before I could stop it.

"Why do you care how I smell?" he countered, the little smirk glowing in one corner of his mouth again and those dusty blue eyes fixed intently on me.

I shook my head. "No, I don't. Sorry. It's just...seriously. Do you eat a lot of licorice?" Now that I'd identified it, I realized I'd been smelling it since we'd walked into the office.

"You like chocolate-covered raisins, I like licorice."

I shrugged. I didn't know many people who actually liked black licorice, but there was something I liked about the smell, not that I was going to tell him that. "How'd you know that, by the way?"

"About the raisins?"

"Yeah."

"Not everyone is clueless," he said. Typical.

"I'm not clueless." Good comeback, Miranda.

"Ever consider that I didn't mean you?" His gaze was boring into me now, and angry heat simmered in his eyes.

I had no idea what to say to that, and found myself scanning back through the last few times I'd seen Sam, trying to figure out when I'd been eating chocolate-covered raisins. They had been my guilty pleasure since I was a kid, but I couldn't remember ever making a big deal about it. That was Sam, though. Latching on to stupid things so he could use them against you someday. No doubt my affinity for chocolate-covered raisins would somehow become a weapon in Sam's hands. Past experience showed that he would hurt me if he could.

Sam blew out a breath and continued. "So every project we've got scheduled is on here." Sam turned his attention back to the spreadsheet. "First I need you to familiarize yourself with the schedule and the plans. Then I need you to do two things. Look at the equipment and manpower resources listed for each job and check them against the lot list and staffing list. Those are over here." He pulled up another sheet in the workbook. "Sometimes Chance books stuff we can't even do because the equipment or people we need are on another job."

I raised my eyebrows, surprised Chance would make a mistake like that. Or any mistake. Chance was perfect as far as I could tell.

"He's not perfect, you know."

Great, now Sam was reading my mind. Heat prickled at my cheeks and the back of my neck, and I couldn't tell if it was from his obvious awareness that I was in love with his brother or if my body was still having some kind of traitorous response to Sam's masculine proximity.

"He's a great salesman, and he's good with the big ideas. Not so good with details."

"Oh." My eyes were running down the spreadsheet, looking for evidence of Sam's statement. Chance was a Stanford MBA. I found it hard to believe he'd be bad at resourcing work.

"The second thing I need is for you to run a total of cost and profit, from these numbers out here." Sam pointed across the screen. "Every job requires investment, and we try to keep payment schedules on track so one client is essentially paying to do work for the next, and the only time we hit the bank is with deposits. Make sense?"

"Sure," I said. I wanted to get to work. The huge screen was packed with numbers and it would take me a while to familiarize myself with the way it was organized. Now that I understood what I was looking at, my mind was turning, eager for the challenge.

"When you've done that, let me know and we'll compare."

Compare? "Wait, you already did this?" I stared at Sam, ignoring his ever-present arrogant smirk.

"Of course."

"So, what? This is some kind of test?" My blood started to boil. Of course it was. Sam was testing me. He didn't think I could manage this job.

Sam let out a sharp breath, clearly frustrated with me and shook his head, a hand rising to rub one side of his jaw. "No. You're just double-checking me, Miranda. I'm not perfect either." He stood and pulled the chair back to the corner of the room. "Answer the phones, too, please."

Sam turned and disappeared into his office, leaving me to decide whether I was angry or not.

Chapter 9

SAM

I couldn't help it. Whenever Miranda walked through the door at Palmer Construction, it was like the air in the office changed. For one thing, she smelled good. Like muffins, or flowers. Or baked flowers. I can't explain it, but I'm used to spending pretty much all my time with my older brother. And while most of the girls I've ever met seem to think Chance smells okay, they didn't grow up sharing a room with the dude. I'm not saying the office normally stinks, nothing like that. And Chance doesn't really stink either, probably. I don't profess to be a dude-smell expert. But I'm saying the air noticeably changes when Miranda arrives—becomes all sunshine and flowers, and I can't help the damned smile that tries to glue itself to my face, or the insane swirl of anticipation in my gut.

Part of it was just something new and different. Not much changed in Kings Grove. Things were a little interesting last year, with all the excitement over Connor Charles. And then Maddie and her brother moved up here, and that was cool. But in general, the locals were the locals, and the place was small.

When I was in high school, I was determined that as soon

as I graduated, I'd be off like a shot. I was going to go to LA, or up to San Francisco. Anywhere there was life and movement, art and culture. New people, new worlds to explore. I wanted the same opportunity Chance had gotten. But then Dad got sick.

The only real consolation to being stuck in this one horse town was Miranda George. And I really couldn't figure out why she was still here. I guess it shouldn't have been much consolation, considering she hated me. But my stupid heart didn't seem to care. Any excuse to be close to Miranda was a good one.

I'd pretty much always felt that way about her, ever since we were in the same class in first grade and she'd tipped over the aquarium on her second day of school. Our teacher, Mr. Aarons, wasn't in the room when it happened—we were supposed to be at lunch, but Miranda forgot something in the room and I came back with her to get it. We peeked in on the fish, and the button on her overalls got caught on the top edge of the aquarium so when she stepped back she pulled the whole thing with her, and it crashed to the floor, fish flopping everywhere and making those sad "o" mouths.

The thing was plastic, so we tipped it back up and tried to arrange the little trees and rocks the way they were. We saved the fish and refilled the whole thing before Mr. Aarons came back. But when he slipped in the massive puddle of water after lunch and found Rocky the goldfish floating belly up the next morning, the jig was up. At recess I told Miranda I'd take the heat. And she almost let me, but that's the thing I love most about her. Miranda has a good heart and a clear view of right and wrong. When I raised my hand and confessed, her blue eyes got wide and watery, and two seconds later she was standing up, telling the whole story.

I might have only been seven years old, but something in my heart recognized it then. That spark she has—that glow inside her that calls to me like some kind of low-frequency dog whistle only I can hear. She's the one. I've thought so for as long as I could remember.

Unfortunately it wasn't mutual. Not even close.

"Doing okay?" I called out to her from my office, unable to just let things be.

"I've been here ten minutes. Nothing I can't handle yet, Sam."

I couldn't help but smile at the sound of her irritation. "Keep me posted." What the hell was wrong with me? I must be a glutton for punishment. It made me happy to have her here, even though it was pretty clear I wasn't her preferred Palmer brother. I hadn't heard her talk to me without that adorable bitey edge of irritation since our freshman year in high school when Miranda had decided to hate me after that party.

I leaned back in my chair and stretched, lacing my fingers behind my neck and staring out the window at the parking lot behind our building. It was full of equipment—backhoes, excavators, dozers. Palmer was doing well, and I was glad to be part of it, even if it did sometimes feel like I was trying to hold up a tent in a hurricane. Chance wasn't the most organized fellow, but he made up in charisma and business development what he lacked in forethought.

The office was quiet for an hour or two, with the exception of me checking in on Miranda and her snapping at me that she was fine and grumbling about my penchant for black licorice. I couldn't help that any more than I could help my admiration for her. I like what I like.

"Seriously, what's the deal? I mean, it'd be one thing if it didn't have such a strong smell." Miranda wrinkled her nose adorably under her glasses, making her entire face scrunch up.

"Anise." I bit the end off the piece of licorice in my hand and chewed it in that adorable way of mine.

"What?" She sighed and leaned back in her chair, giving me an exasperated look.

"The smell. It's anise. It's some kind of herb or flower or something."

"I hate it."

I lifted a shoulder. "I'll add it to the list," I told her. "Sure you don't want a piece?"

She sat back up abruptly. "Seriously? No!" She made a point of giving her full attention to the screen in front of her again, clearly dismissing me.

I would have been put off by Miranda's clear message of disdain for me if we hadn't had such a long shared history. I knew she had a good heart. And one day maybe she'd forgive me for something that really hadn't been my fault.

"Reminds me of my dad," I told her, leaning against the doorframe between my office and the reception area.

She dropped her hands from the keyboard with a sigh and her eyes slowly rose to meet mine. "Now I remind you of your dad?" Her voice was wavering between irritation and all-out anger.

"Not you," I laughed. "The licorice. When I came in here as a kid, my dad always had a bag of black licorice in his top desk drawer. I remember him chewing on it while he worked in there." I nodded toward my own desk, and for a split second, I could see my dad there just like he'd been back in the day, his hat pulled down over his brow as he pored over papers on the desk with a piece of licorice hanging from his lips. "He started eating it when Chance was born, because Mom made him quit smoking."

Miranda's face had changed, and she didn't look as pissed. I gave her a sad smile. Talking about Dad and Mom always made my heart hurt a little.

"Your dad was a great man," she said softly.

Hearing her say the words made my heart hurt even more,

and part of me felt like I might actually cry if I just stood there looking at her. I'm sure she'd think that was pretty attractive. I laughed instead. "He was. So the licorice stays. It's a tribute. And a habit."

"I'll get used to it," she said, her voice less angry than it had been earlier. "I've been comparing the lists like you asked," she said, her voice becoming more businesslike, like she'd pushed a button and switched it. "And there are a couple things that don't line up."

I walked around the desk and peered at the screen in front of Miranda, trying not to be distracted by the faint lemon scent of her hair or the fact that if I leaned in just a little more I could bury my nose in it. She had both documents up, side by side, and had highlighted inconsistencies so I could clearly see where the errors were. Smart girl.

"Here," she pointed at the screen. "This truck went in for repairs and then was retired, right?"

"Backhoe."

"Backhoe yourself," she said, annoyance creeping back into her voice. "You see what I'm talking about here? This truck." she jabbed the screen.

"Yeah, you're right. But it's a backhoe, not a truck."

She turned and stared at me, understanding clearing the anger in her eyes and making them dance. "Oh. Right. Okay. Backhoe. I thought you were..."

"I'm not calling you a backhoe," I assured her. I hadn't dropped to the name-calling level yet. Give me a few more days dealing with the crazy nerves being close to Miranda inspired, though, and anything was possible.

I stepped back, forcing some distance between myself and the lemon scent that made me want to wrap my arms around the girl in front of me. I cleared my throat, aware of the blood racing through my body. "That's good," I said. My voice sounded weird, but I forced myself to think about backhoes and bobcats. "Can you just make a list of the discrepancies? I'll see if we have enough for the jobs we've got planned or if we might have to shift the schedule around a bit to free up resources from other jobs."

"Sure," she said.

"Hey, look who's hard at work!" Chance said, bursting through the door in his usual whirlwind.

Miranda's back noticeably straightened. "Hi," she said softly.

But Chance was already bustling into his office, dropping blueprints and his laptop onto his desk. "Sam," he called. "Can I talk to you, bro?"

"Yeah, I'm standing right behind you." I'd followed him into his office, but as was his nature, he was unaware of it. After all, I was not him. And while Chance was a good guy, the only person who really interested him fully was…him.

"Ah, yeah. How's it going here? With…" he pointed a thumb to the outer office at Miranda. I was glad she couldn't see him. Everything about his posture felt dismissive of her.

"Really good," I said, fully aware that Miranda could hear every word I said. "Miranda's smart and quick. She's already identified a couple discrepancies with the resourcing for the jobs coming up in the next month."

Chance stopped his whirlwind of motion and dropped his palms to his desk. "Nope. Just looked at that list yesterday, we're good."

I raised an eyebrow at my brother. "She's just double-checking."

"I don't need to be double-checked, man. I did it last night, and we're solid."

"The old backhoe went in for servicing and didn't come out, remember? We talked to Tony about retiring it last week, but you've got it scheduled for two weeks up at the Honor Dam development."

Miranda appeared at my shoulder. "I'll check again," she said, her voice totally different when Chance was around than it was when she spoke to me. "Maybe I missed something."

"You didn't," I bit out, still watching my brother. I didn't like her apologizing for doing good work.

Chance shrugged and shot Miranda his best panty-melting smile. "Nah," he said. "It was probably my mistake. No big deal."

I watched Miranda's face as Chance's smile did its work. Target acquired, locked, and ... direct hit. She melted and went back to her desk, a faint smile still on her face.

That was Chance. Our whole lives he'd gotten away with everything, skated by on looks and charm. That's not to say he wasn't smart—he was. Smart enough to know that in this world, looks and charm would get you pretty damned far. We had more clients than we could handle, thanks to my brother's looks and charm. And I hoped Miranda might really be able to help me shoulder the mountain of work that created back here at the office.

CHANCE SETTLED IN AFTER A WHILE—HE always took about fifteen minutes of hurricaning around the office to finally become productive again. For him, that meant shutting his door and making calls while I poured over spreadsheets full of payroll and logistics details. Not to make it sound unfair or anything—I also drew the plans. And that part was my favorite. But you draw the plans for a project, and once the client approves them, that's that, with the exception of a few modifications here and there. And what remains is all the less fun stuff. Spreadsheets, like I said.

"Sam, I'm ready to take my test," Miranda said, standing at my door.

She found me at my drafting desk, in one of those rare moments when I wasn't doing what I should have been doing.

"What's this?" she said, stepping to my side and glancing around me to see the drawing I was working on.

I pulled a blueprint from the side of the table and slid it over the top of my landscape, well aware she'd already seen it.

"Nothing, just screwing around." My voice was harsher than I'd intended and she recoiled, stepping away. I straightened and moved back a step, and Miranda reached over and slid the landscape out again, almost spitefully, like she thought she was going to catch me doing something horrible.

Her face rearranged as she took in the image I'd drawn—a pastoral view of a meadow with the shadow of the ridge out behind it. She went from looking agitated or angry to something calmer, almost reverent. "This is good, Sam." She sounded shocked I might be capable of anything besides sarcasm.

"Great. Thanks for the endorsement." I hated the biting tone I heard in my own voice, and I swallowed hard and turned to face her. Since she'd been reaching around me, the move practically put her in my embrace. Her arm grazed my side as I spun and she stood inches from my chest, the crown of her blond head just below my chin. At that range, I could smell her shampoo again and I had to restrain myself from wrapping my arms around her waist and pulling her into me. Every cell in my body wanted to see what that would feel like, to have her against me, to bury my face in that sweet scent of hers, to have the chance to hold her, kiss her.

But as quickly as I'd spun, she stepped backward with a surprised "oh," and the space where she'd been was left with only a shadow of her presence as she moved to the other side of the room. I cleared my throat and turned to quickly adjust myself without her noticing. Having Miranda George inches away was almost unbearable, and my body was responding as if the thought of touching her might be anything more than a dream.

"So the numbers?" she said, her voice less certain than it had been before. "Your little test?"

"Right." I picked up the printout I'd made of the spreadsheet I'd had her looking at. "And it isn't a test. I told you. We make mistakes. Having another set of eyes can help prevent that."

"Uh-huh." She didn't believe me at all.

I followed her to the reception area and pulled a chair up to her desk. She scooted away from me, the wheels of the old secretary chair squealing as she forced them sideways. "Only a couple things besides that backhoe. Here," she pointed at the screen. "And here."

I dropped my eyes to my own spreadsheet. I'd only caught one of those, but she was on target. "Yeah, you're right. Dammit."

"Is it that hard to accept I'm not a complete moron?"

I dropped the spreadsheet on the desk and looked up at her, catching her narrowed blue eyes and the stiff defensive posture of her body, leaning as far from me as she could get. She really hated me. Worse, it was clear she didn't trust me. Not that I'd ever given her much of a reason to—I'd never explained that I'd also been a victim in that incident in the shed, and then I'd been immature and rude to avoid being humiliated in the wake of revealing anything close to my actual feelings. Her body language made me think of a caged animal, pulling itself to the far reaches of its cage to get away from its captor.

"Miranda," I said, my voice almost a whisper. It made my heart hurt to have to see up close how much she reviled me. Especially because I felt so differently about her. I'd spent years trying to get past the ridiculous crush I had on her, but it'd been pointless, and now I'd grown used to the dull ache I felt when she wasn't around, and the sharp intense pain of her disdain when she was. Add to that the crushing jealousy I fought off when I watched her moon over my brother, and I was a pretty solid mess. "I don't think you're a moron. I'm not trying to trick you or trap you …" I spread my hands across my thighs and tried to figure out how to talk to someone who distrusted me so completely. "Listen, you and me…we used to be friends—"

"That's ancient history, Sam," she interrupted.

"I know. And I know I screwed things up. I know it was that party, and then the prom—"

"I'm not talking about that." Her chin lifted and her shoulders tensed even more as she shut the door on the apology I was about to offer for not telling her what had really happened at that party that had ended up with us both in the shed. Or for doing exactly the wrong thing at the prom.

"Okay, fine." My mind was spinning. This was not going well, and I couldn't have her here if it was going to disrupt business, or make me a complete babbling buffoon when I needed to be the one to keep this enterprise in the black. "Look. I need you here. We need you here. In one day you've proven your value, and I know now that I can trust you to help me keep the resources and numbers on track. That's more than Chance can do…"

"Chance is—"

"You don't need to defend my brother." I felt suddenly exhausted, watching the fire jump into her eyes as she prepared to defend Chance. I heard the defeat in my voice as I spoke the next part. "He's important here, too. He's the face of the company, the guy who brings in the work. Sometimes he even does some of the work."

She raised an angry eyebrow.

When would I learn that sarcasm and Miranda George were not a good match?

I sighed, rubbing a hand over my jaw. *Try again, Sam. Get it right.* "I'm trying to say that we need you here. And I'm also trying to thank you for what you've done already today. I might've been testing you a bit, but it's only because this is our family legacy, and I need to protect it. I wanted to be sure you could handle the responsibilities I want to throw at you."

"I really thought you just needed someone to answer phones." She sounded less defensive. That was progress, at least.

I shrugged a shoulder, glancing at Chance's closed door. "That's what Chance thought. But he doesn't see the churn that happens outside his orbit of awesomeness. There's a lot of gritwork, and I need help. Are you up for that?"

Miranda glanced at Chance's door too, a wistful expression crossing her face before it hardened again as she turned back to me. "Yes. But not a single mention of the past from you." She put a finger in my chest.

I couldn't help the little grin that stretched my cheeks at her touch. She was adorable when she was trying to be threatening. "You mean I can't talk about the aquarium?"

"No."

"Or the time we were playing hide and seek and it started pouring rain and you left me out there forever while you went in to get hot chocolate?"

"That either."

I was enjoying this. Her cheeks had turned a glorious shade of pink and her eyes were flashing behind her frames. If I couldn't have anything else from her, at least I had history. I wasn't giving it up. "What about that time at the dance—"

"I'm not kidding, Sam. I don't ever want to talk about that."

She thought I was talking about prom again. But that hadn't been my intention. "I wasn't talking about that. I was thinking of eighth grade, when—"

"Enough." She looked at her watch. "It's five. What time am I off?"

"Five." I said, feeling my chest deflate as she stood and went to the tall cabinet to pick up her purse. "But Miranda, one day we will have to talk about all that, you know. One day you'll have to let me apologize. To clear the air."

"There's no apology needed. We were young, and you were an idiot."

"Well, I don't know if idiot is the right word," I began, unable to keep my mouth from leaping to defend my ego.

"Whatever," she sniffed. "See you in the morning. My shift at the diner is tomorrow afternoon, so I'll come here first."

And just like that, she was gone. Gone and pissed off at me. Pretty much the description of the last ten years when it came to me and Miranda.

Chapter 10
MIRANDA

My first day at Palmer Construction wasn't exactly a raging success. On the other hand, I hadn't broken anything, spilled anything on anyone, or screwed up the work I'd been asked to do. But the day had not gone according to my fantasy about it either. In the fantasy, Chance had opened the door for me and sat on the edge of my desk while I made keen observations about their need to expand beyond construction and into interiors so that I could be made a full partner in the business. Sometimes in the fantasy, Chance would tell me that now that I was there, we wouldn't need Sam at all. And then Sam would leave town as Chance and I stood arm in arm waving goodbye to him. Sam Palmer would drive away and take all his teasing and prodding and stirring up of the past with him. And then there'd be the steamy kiss with Chance.

But that wasn't how my first day had gone at all, and I wasn't sure if spending my time side by side with Sam Palmer would be made bearable by the mere possibility of getting a little time with Chance. I doubted it very much.

Beyond the Palmers, though, I'd found a glimmer of something else while I'd sat behind that big desk, poring over numbers and plans. I'd found it challenging and enjoyable, even with the ever-present licorice scent wafting around me, making me feel like a detainee in Willy Wonka's black vine prison. The work—it had been good. And interesting.

At home that night, I'd told my parents about it, and they'd smiled as I gushed about having found a couple errors, about doing something more productive than pouring coffee and delivering waffles.

"That's great, pudding," Dad said, ruffling my hair and taking the seat next to me at the round table we used for everything. "And you'll still have time to study?" He glanced out to where the new computer sat, its big screen beckoning me near.

"Definitely." And with that, I rose and reseated myself in front of the Mac I'd saved a year to buy. The computer that would allow me to get my design degree, and could support the software needed to do the actual work.

"Morning," Sam called as I pulled open the front door of Palmer Construction the following morning. Even a greeting sounded like a taunt, coming from him.

I pushed down my potentially unreasonable annoyance, and called back, "Good morning!"

And then it was as if the clouds parted and the sun washed me new in the glory of its rays. Chance Palmer stepped into the room, his smile bright and his amazing grey-blue eyes fixed on me. "Miranda!" he said. And he sounded happy to see me.

Being the focus of Chance's singular attention, even for a brief morning greeting, was almost enough to drop me flat. My heart took off at a gallop, my palms got sweaty, and my dress suddenly felt tight. All my clothes actually felt awkward. Or maybe it was that my body had suddenly slicked with sweat, and everything was sticky and uncomfortable. I couldn't hold his eyes, and dropped them, only to find my gaze lingering down the length of his body, pausing a beat too long in the one spot you really shouldn't be caught staring at on a man. I gulped hard and tore my eyes away, grabbing at my purse and then pretending to check my phone before stupidly uttering something about my mother.

So smooth.

I stumbled around my desk, pushing my purse into the tall cabinet, and then turned back around, hating the heat I felt in my cheeks. Both Sam and Chance were standing in front of my desk, watching me. Sam turned to look at his brother, and I imagined the thoughts going through his head. *What an idiot. She's such a klutz!* Chance, for his part, just looked surprised.

"Well," he said, his eyebrows rising high over those fathomless eyes as he wiped his hands across the front of his jeans. "I'm excited to see more great things from you this week, Miranda. Sam told me all about the stuff you caught yesterday. Nice job!"

"S-s-sure," I stammered.

"You comfortable enough out here? Need anything?" he asked, leaning on the side of my desk. A scent of cologne wafted my way, something woodsy and touched with something more esoteric, like unicorn sweat. It smelled like heaven.

"All good," I said, noticing that I'd begun salivating heavily.

God, how could I imagine a future with him if I couldn't even be near him without my body going into some kind of pheromone-fueled overload that turned me stupid, speechless, and drooly? This was impossible.

"I got her all set up," Sam said, stepping closer. Now licorice was added to the heady mix of scents and my head felt like it was swimming.

"Just checking," Chance said, giving me his killer smile again.

Sam crossed his arms and looked annoyed, and I got the sense again that things were not always peaceful here at Palmer —not between them, at least.

"So, Miranda," Chance said, his voice just above a whisper, the syllables dripping over me like warm honey. "I have a favor to ask."

I found myself nodding, not caring what he was going to ask, ready to do anything this man wanted.

He dropped a Post-It note in front of me. "Can you send flowers to this address?" He dropped his chin and then gave me a half-smile, looking sheepish. "I should have sent them a week ago, so I'd appreciate it if you could make them something special. Use the card in the desk."

"What?" Sam said, his voice louder than usual. "That's not why she's here, Romeo. Handle your own apologies, loser." He picked up the Post-It, on which I'd noticed the name *Christine*, and flung it back at him.

Chance stood up straight and spread his arms in a shrug that made him seem innocent. "What?"

"Miranda's too smart to spend her time answering phones and ordering flowers for your one-night stands, Chance. Do it yourself."

I sat up straighter, not sure at what point in this exchange I should speak up, if at all. I was torn. I was happy to do whatever Chance asked of me—like anything, really. But at the same time, my heart was sinking to hear mention of other women in his life. Women who'd gotten to touch that long strong body. Women who'd gotten to press their lips to his, to feel his hands on them ... Women who were not me.

"It's okay," I offered, but the men were facing each other in a standoff, both of them silent. Finally, Chance turned and strode into his office and closed the door. Just as Sam turned to say something to me, the door opened again and Chance walked back out, his car keys and a laptop case in hand.

"Just remembered I have some work to do in the valley," he said. "Be back tomorrow."

I watched him leave, my chest tightening slightly at the knowledge that I'd been involved in the event that had made Chance so upset. I hoped he wouldn't hold it against me.

Once he'd left, Sam stood silently in front of my desk for a few long seconds, staring at the floor. He seemed to be deep in thought, so I just left him there and got started pulling up the documents we'd been looking at the day before. I'd almost managed to forget he was there when he sighed heavily and dropped his hands onto my desk across from me.

"Miranda," he said.

I narrowed my eyes at him. The tone of his voice suggested I would not like what he was about to say.

"Do you want my help?"

"With what?" I asked, unable to keep the suspicion from creeping into my voice.

"With my brother."

"Wait, I'm not sure I get it." Maddie's eyes were wide as she leaned against the counter with her arms crossed, listening to me explain Sam's offer.

"I don't know if I do either, but he said he'd help me get Chance's attention."

Maddie didn't say anything, but her eyes narrowed and her nose scrunched up a bit, so I could tell she was thinking about something.

"What?"

She shrugged. "That's pretty nice of him," she said.

"Yeah, but I don't trust him. The guy lives to see me humiliate myself." About four hundred examples flew through my mind.

"Sam seems like a trustworthy guy, actually."

"That's because you haven't known him since kindergarten." When I thought of Sam, my blood heated in fury over all the times he'd been right there with an evil comment when the most humiliating events of my life had happened. He'd been a witness to practically every single flub, and it was hard not to associate him, or even blame him. And I did blame him for some of it.

"True." Maddie turned as the bell over the door rang and Adele greeted Cameron, Maddie's brother.

"Well, if it isn't my very favorite Turner!" Adele patted Cameron's arm and beamed at him. No one could figure out why her attitude reversed so completely when Cam was around, but he seemed to be the only person in town she actually liked, besides Frank.

"Good to see you, Adele," Cameron said, leaning over to kiss her jowly cheek. He turned and Maddie went to meet him.

"I heard that comment, by the way," Maddie said to Adele. "And my feelings are a little hurt."

Adele waved this away with a sigh and a flapping hand. "You're made of steel, nothing hurts you. Besides you're not really a Turner anyway. You're practically a Charles."

Cam came to sit at the counter and I put a cup of coffee in front of him, sliding it carefully and only slopping a few drops over the edge onto the saucer. "Hey Miranda." Cam had a soft spoken way about him, despite his tough looks. He'd had a shaved head and a goatee when I'd first met him, but he'd let his almost black hair grow back, and with the facial hair, he had kind of a Grizzly Adams thing happening.

"You've gotta do something about this," Maddie said, fingering the overlong hair.

Cam ignored her. "Not high on my list."

I couldn't help feeling sorry for Cameron. He'd come to Kings Grove when Maddie was first dating Connor, with his adorable wife in tow, and the love between those two had practically shone in the air around them. Unfortunately, his wife Jess was sick, and she'd passed away. That was why Cam had moved up here from Los Angeles, leaving the movie industry behind to work construction jobs with the Palmer brothers. He often stayed silent, his sad dark eyes full of a pain I could only begin to imagine. I knew it was wrong, but part of me wished for a man who'd mourn me as devotedly if I were to die as Cameron mourned his late wife, Jess. I doubted he'd ever look at another woman.

"What can I get you?" Maddie asked him, and I moved off to check on my other tables.

Maddie and Cam chatted over the counter while he ate a sandwich, and a little while later, my dad came through the door, dusty and dirty as always.

"Family day seems to be happening over at the counter," Adele said, her surly mood returning.

"Hey pudding," Dad said, grabbing a stool next to Cam. "Cameron, Maddie," he said.

"How's the rangering?" Cameron asked him.

Dad put his hat on the counter next to him and shook his head, not answering right away. Something inside me prickled with concern. "Not that good right now," he said, and an all-out worry blossomed inside my chest.

"What's going on?" I asked, dropping my order pad to the counter where it missed the edge and slid immediately to the floor. I leaned down to get it, banging my head on the way down, and replaced the pad in my apron pocket, rubbing my forehead. That was probably going to bruise.

Dad waited for me to finish injuring myself and then explained. "The fire over the back ridge is still growing. We're getting a little worried about it since none of the predicted storms have materialized and crews are having a hard time getting a perimeter set up because the canyons back there are so steep. If the wind would stop, that'd be one thing, but between the Santa Anas and all the dry fuel on the ground …" he trailed off, shaking his head.

"How far away is it?" Cam asked.

"I don't think we need to worry about it here quite yet," Dad said.

"Yet?" Maddie's voice had gone thin with worry.

"They'll get it under control," Dad said, but I could hear the uncertainty in his voice.

Adele cleared her throat, moving Maddie and I back out to the dining area, where Dean had begun servicing a few tables as the early dinner rush got underway. For a couple hours I was too busy to think about Sam's offer or the fire threatening the backcountry, but as I wrapped up my shift, Maddie took my arm.

"Are you going to let him do it?" she asked.

"What? Who?"

"Sam. Are you going to let him help you get Chance's attention?"

I shrugged. I hadn't had time to decide. "I don't know. No one knows Chance better than Sam, right?"

She nodded. "Still, don't you wonder a little bit why he'd be willing?"

I did. Sam had never done anything but go out of his way to humiliate me. "Yeah, a little."

"You don't think maybe Sam has a little crush on you, do you?" she asked. "I mean, I've seen the way he watches you."

"I'm just the local entertainment, Maddie. It's been that way forever." Sam wouldn't know a crush if it smacked him in the face, and if he had one, it certainly wouldn't be on me.

"He's pretty hot, you know." She looked thoughtful, her eyes darkening. "And I feel a little sorry for him, actually."

I felt my eyes widen. "Who, Sam? Why in the world would you feel sorry for him?"

She pressed her lips together and shook her head lightly. "I don't know, in Chance's shadow and everything. Can't be easy."

An exasperated sigh escaped my lips. I didn't think Sam needed any sympathy. "I don't think he cares." As soon as I'd said it, my mind rolled back to the confrontation I'd witnessed in the office that morning, and to the resigned way Sam had talked about the divided responsibilities they each shouldered at work. Maybe he did care a little. But if he was willing to help me finally get his brother's attention, I was going to let him.

There wasn't a single part of me that felt sorry for Sam Palmer.

Even if I did kind of agree that he was a little bit hot.

Chapter 11
MIRANDA

When I arrived to Palmer Construction the following morning, I was wearing a pair of fitted black pants and a peplum blouse, and I'd left my hair down, even though it drove me nuts. I wasn't used to the feel of it against the back of my neck, and I swear there'd been a point while I ate breakfast where I'd thought there was some kind of bug crawling on my arm, only to discover it was my own hair. I'd screamed and jumped out of my seat, smacking at my arm and flinging my cereal spoon across the table at Mom. Once I'd finished freaking out, my mother had suggested it might be a good plan to put my hair up while I ate to prevent myself making a mess at mealtime.

"That's not necessary, Mom." I stood by my statement, but my spilled cereal told a different story. Mom had sighed and gone to get a cloth to wipe up the spill.

Despite my unfamiliarity with my own hair, I believed I was looking halfway decent that morning, and hoped Chance might notice too. I didn't know what Sam had planned for me work-wise—probably more stuff he'd already done himself so he could find places where I'd screwed up—but I'd spent some time researching the project the Palmers had just finished down in the valley. It was a strip mall renovation, and the new buildings had a really unique facade—not low and boxy like most strip malls, but each store had a little patio or garden in front, and the actual architecture varied dramatically from shop to shop, so the result was more like an old fashioned downtown sidewalk than a strip mall. Sam might have designed it, but Chance had made it happen—even though the locals had put up a stink about it being too "unusual" to fit in with their town. Chance had charmed them into submission—the man was a genius. The project had even won a couple awards. I knew all about it, and was ready to engage in pithy construction-based conversation.

"Morning, Miranda." Sam stood in the middle of the front office, facing his brother's door. He turned toward me as he greeted me, and the smile that crossed his face transformed him for a split second. I almost forgot how much he irritated me. His dark hair was tousled and he had a scruff of a beard, like he'd forgotten to shave for a couple days. His flannel shirt was rolled up at the sleeves and only half tucked into the khaki jeans he wore, and even though Sam Palmer always reverted in my mind to the guy I needed to be wary of and careful around, there was a weird uncomfortable moment that morning when the alertness I always felt around him morphed into nerves at being faced with such an attractive man. His shoulders were broad and his torso narrowed down into a perfect vee, and the way his pants hung on his hips and thighs made them look so strong and muscular.

Get a grip, I told myself. It's Sam.

The thing was—even though I'd reminded myself it was Sam, I still found him handsome. I wondered for a second if maybe the way he'd defended my intelligence to Chance had somehow made up for some of his past indiscretions. Or if his offer to help me get his brother's attention had made me subconsciously like him more. Maybe there was a strange Miranda-Sam power balance inside me somewhere, and his recent uncharacteristic behavior had shifted things slightly back to center. I still didn't trust him not to say something awful at any second, though.

I cleared my throat and said, "Hi Sam," and then moved around my desk to put my purse away.

Sam turned and his eyes widened slightly and then traveled down the length of me and back up, the blue-gray orbs dark and clouded as he did so. "I'd tell you that you look nice today, but that'd probably be inappropriate," he said.

I wasn't sure what I was supposed to say to that. "Okay." I hadn't gotten a chance to look and see if his brother was in his office, but I'd seen his truck out front. "Hi Chance," I ventured.

Six feet of rugged handsomeness appeared in the doorway. "Miranda," Chance said. His gorgeous eyes landed on me and my face was immediately flaming.

I accidentally giggled, but covered by clearing my throat. Which led to an uncomfortable tickle as something in my throat got jostled the wrong way, and suddenly I was coughing uncontrollably, gripping the edge of the desk. Dammit. I didn't want to die choking on my own spit in front of Chance Palmer.

"You okay?" Sam came around the desk and put a hand on my back. I was coughing too hard to shake him off.

I nodded my head, but when I kept coughing, Sam pounded the hand on my back and sent me lurching forward, bending almost in half over the desk.

"Hey!" I managed as my coughing fit faded. "You just clobbered me!"

"Sorry, thought you were dying." Sam shrugged and gave me the annoying little-boy grin he'd been wearing since we were six. "Didn't mean to whack you so hard."

Chance was grinning at me like he thought this entire

episode was either charming or downright hilarious. I was going with charming. I pushed my hair behind my ears and stood up straight, using one hand to wipe my chin in case spit might be sliding down it. "So what's going on today?" I asked, trying my best to look put together and professional.

"We're scheduled to do a site survey for the Allen's new cabin," Sam said. He ran a hand over his forehead as he stepped back to the other side of my desk, making a face I couldn't identify. "But I'm really not feeling that well." He made another face, scrunching his mouth and nose together like he smelled something awful. I wondered if he'd finally realized that black licorice was disgusting—a vague scent of the spicy sweet clung to him again this morning. I'd noticed it when he came around to slug me a minute before.

"What's wrong, little bro? Too many beers last night?" Chance didn't look worried about his brother. He turned to me, "Little guy can't hold his liquor. Never could."

I had no idea what to say to that, so I just nodded. Neither of the Palmers were "little guys" and I got the distinct sense Chance used this term to subtly put his brother down, and that didn't fit with my good-guy image of him. An unfamiliar dislike prickled in me.

"Well, anyway," Sam said, holding his stomach now and backing toward the door. "I think I'd better go home. You two will have to handle things on your own this morning."

Chance sighed and stepped out to face me as Sam put a hand on the front door. "We've got this, right Miranda? We'll head over to the Allen's in fifteen minutes."

A thrill ran through me, both at being directly addressed by Chance, and at the thought of working right next to him today. Plus, if we were going to the Allen's, I'd get to sit next to him in a car—that'd be closer than I'd ever been to Chance, with the exception of the time when he caught me after I'd tripped off the curb in the parking lot last winter. Or the time he'd put his arm around me at prom—but then I'd been too ashamed and humiliated to enjoy it.

Sam pulled the door open and turned back to face me. Chance had gone back into his office and didn't see it when Sam gave me two thumbs up and a wink, whispering too loudly, "Go get him, tiger."

I made a face at Sam, realizing he wasn't sick at all. As the door to the office closed and I took my place behind the desk, I understood that Sam had engineered a day for me to be alone with Chance. The question now was, what was I going to do?

I had to be calm, and I needed to let Chance see that I was mature and intelligent, too. The more I contemplated what I might possibly talk about with him on the upcoming car ride, the more nervous I became. I was so focused on my own thoughts, the ringing phone made me jump.

"Palmer Construction," I said, answering the main line.

"You're welcome," came a deep familiar voice. Sam.

"Thank you?" I said, ceding the point. When he'd said he was going to 'help' me, I'd imagined some useful tips, but I guessed this worked too. "Any advice?" I asked, second-guessing myself a bit for giving Sam an opening. I generally tried not to be vulnerable in front of him, but this situation had turned everything on its side.

"Sure. So my brother is completely self-absorbed. Just focus the conversation on him, and he'll adore you."

"Is that real advice or are you just being an ass?" I whispered, turning away from Chance's office.

Sam chuckled on the other end of the line. "I guess you'll find out," he said. Something in his voice sounded sad, but despite Maddie's suggestion that I might feel sorry for Sam, I wasn't going to ask him why. The fact that he was doing anything to help me was shocking enough. "Good luck," he said.

"Thanks," I managed.

Just after I'd hung up, Chance stepped into his doorway, his solid wide shoulders filling the space. "Ready?" He wore a plaid flannel shirt, similar to the one Sam had on this morning, but on Chance it was like wearing a tuxedo. It enhanced the color of his eyes, made the little hollow point at the base of his throat look positively lickable where it was framed by the soft fabric on either side, and made his tanned muscular forearms look like they were carved from some dark expensive stone. He was almost too perfect looking, if that was even possible. I could barely breathe, let alone form a word, so I just stood nodding my assent.

It occurred to me that I was supposed to be helping in some way, but I had no idea what my job would be in relation to a site survey. "What do I need to bring?" I asked, glad to have a task to focus on.

"Something to record notes and measurements," Chance said, tucking a pencil next to his ear as he grabbed a toolbox from the floor next to the cabinet. "I've got most of what we'll need in the truck." He opened a cupboard and pulled something out, then placed it on my desk. "Here, you be in charge of this," he said.

It was a fancy digital camera, the kind with removable lenses and delicate parts that I suspected were easily broken. *Oh jeez.* "Okay," I said, picking it up and pulling the strap around my neck. The camera hung in front of my chest and I realized I probably just looked like a wayward tourist, so I quickly pulled it back off, slinging it over one shoulder instead.

Chance watched all this with amusement. "Ready to go there, George?"

Oh God, he couldn't call me George. I hated my last name. Kids in high school had all called me George, and it had been the perfect clumsy oafy name to go with my clumsy oafy ways. "Call me Miranda," I managed to say.

Chance was holding the door open for me, and he smiled

when I said this as if I'd told him a joke. "Sure, sorry about that."

We went outside and I got into the passenger side of the Palmer Construction truck, holding my breath as Chance climbed in beside me. When he shot me a winning grin and then pulled a pair of sunglasses from the dash, my heart nearly stopped. How could one man be so handsome?

WE MET Abraham Allen on a lot at the far eastern edge of the village, where his family had owned a cabin for almost a hundred years. The original structure had been modified through the years—only in that it now had an indoor bathroom (though the outhouse still stood, leaning, up the hillside), and the walls were enclosed. The earliest cabins up here had been tented sleeping platforms with separate kitchen tents. My own house had begun that way. Most of the cabins got upgraded and modified over the generations, and a lot of them were as modern as any house in the valley at this point. But Mr. Allen hadn't done much to the structures his great grandfather had originally erected, and now he hoped to change that.

"Hey Abe, how are you?" Chance greeted the older man with a handshake and another of his winning smiles. I wondered if the smile had the same effect on Abe Allen that it had on me, but since he seemed capable of responding, I guessed the answer was no.

"Good, Chance. Hey Miranda. You doing construction now? Don't think those are the right shoes for the job." Abe laughed at his own joke, and all three of us looked down at where the soft hillside dirt now crept into the toes of my sandals, turning my toes a lovely shade of dirt brown and gathering at the edges of my pale pink toenails.

I felt the flush creep up my neck. "Didn't know I'd be

outside the office today," I said, glancing quickly at Chance.

"We like to keep her guessing," Chance said, still chuckling. "We'll get you some steel-toed boots before we get you working demolition, okay?" As he said this, Chance threw his arm around my shoulders and pulled me tightly in to his side. It was a friendly gesture that went with his joke, but it nearly sent me to the ground in a puddle. My heart tried to fly out of my chest and I was pretty sure all the blood in my body had flooded into the points on my right side where Chance's hard body was making contact with my own.

God, he felt like he was made out of steel. And he was so tall, and warm, and ... oh God, there was that heady smell again. I loved his cologne. As Chance let me go and I struggled not to fall over, I was surprised to find my mind noticing the absence of anise. Almost wishing for it? Which was crazy, because I hated it.

Abe and Chance had begun walking the property, and once I'd recovered from Chance's...hug? Could I call that a hug? In my memories it would definitely be a hug. I scrambled to keep up.

"The laws about renovation are a little complicated up here," Chance was saying as Abe waved his arms around, telling Chance what he wanted to build. "Because the entire village is considered historic, you aren't supposed to obscure the original structure, demo it, or add anything out of scale with it."

Abe stopped walking and stared at Chance. "So you're telling me I can shine up these two little sheds and that's it?"

Chance laughed and patted Abe's back with a wink. "Nah, we've got a few tricks up our sleeve." He pulled out a measuring tape and began barking out numbers, which I managed to write down as he said them. He stopped every few minutes to sketch something on a pad, and after about fifteen minutes, he walked back to where Abraham had sat on a tree stump to watch. "How about something like this?" He showed the pad to Abe and I stepped behind him, gazing over the older man's head.

Chance had drawn a two-story house, with the existing small sheds sticking out on either side like wings. It looked nice, still a bit rustic, but I wasn't sure he hadn't just broken the rules he'd spouted off a few minutes before.

"Yeah, I mean … can we do that?" Abe asked.

Chance laughed. "Yeah, we can do that." He looked around the property, which sat on a significant slope. "We'll need to level things up, dig in the foundation between the two existing buildings …" he seemed to be thinking. "Yep, no problem."

"How long will it take?"

"I bet we can have it up by Christmas," Chance said, and my mind spun. I'd seen the list of projects they already had lined up and was pretty sure most of the crews and equipment were booked through at least September. I knew next to nothing about construction, but wondered how this was possible.

"Wow," I said, not meaning to speak out loud.

Chance shot me a glance with narrowed eyes. It could potentially have been translated to "shhhh." But I didn't read narrowed-eye glances very well.

"That seems fast," I said. "The bulk of the crews are on other jobs until the fall—you could probably get a few guys in and out for a couple days between jobs. But what do you do if we get an early snow?"

"She's new," Chance laughed, turning to me. His eyes weren't narrowed now, but the blue gray had darkened, and he definitely didn't look happy with me.

I smiled and wished I could suck the words back in.

"We can hire a new crew, Abe," Chance said, "and the odds of an early snow are slim based on recent years."

My dad put a bit of stock in the Farmer's Almanac, which was actually predicting early snow this year, but it didn't seem like a good idea to mention that now. A tiny cloud of shame was expanding inside me. Why had I said anything? I wasn't a construction expert.

"I see," Abe was saying.

"Miranda," Chance turned to me, his face open and smiling again. "Why don't you grab some shots while we're here? Get the old structures on all four sides, and some good wide shots of the land around the buildings, okay?"

I held up the camera in response, the way a chimpanzee might indicate that it understood a command. Realizing I was a moron, I lowered the camera and turned down my ridiculous grin to a moderate smile. "Sure," I said, cringing at my own inability to behave like a normal person around Chance, and still feeling ashamed after his reprimand.

After we'd said goodbye to Abe, we headed back to the office, Chance's heady smell surrounding me in the small cab of the truck. He didn't speak for a few minutes as we bumped down the narrow potholed roads of the village. As we neared the office again, he looked over at me. "Hey, Miranda. I know you're new to construction. So it'd be really great if you'd just be eyes and ears for a while, okay?"

Gah. I wanted to disappear. "I know, Chance, I'm really sorry about that," I said, my words rushing out. "I just...I'd been looking at the resourcing the other day, and it just popped into my head, and—"

"Right," he interrupted. "And that's cool. It's just … you know, don't say stuff like that in front of someone who wants to pay us to tell them what they want to hear, okay?"

"But you *can* actually do the work by Christmas?"

He laughed. "No, probably not. I mean, Sam will tell me. He's the numbers guy. I just bring in the jobs."

"But you told Abe you could," I said, remembering the glee

on the older man's face as he probably imagined planning a white Christmas in his new house.

"Construction is notoriously off-schedule," Chance said. "He won't be surprised."

I closed my open mouth and turned back to gaze out the windshield. I didn't like that. I didn't like the way Chance just accepted that he'd be disappointing a man who trusted him. "Okay," I said. And just as I thought maybe Chance wasn't the guy I'd always believed him to be, he saved it.

"Miranda," he said, fixing those piercing eyes on me as we parked in front of the office again. "I love seeing your commitment to our clients, and your worry for them. The way you look out for other people," he smiled and shook his head. "It's one of the things I love most about you."

Loved? He loved things about me?

"And I want to assure you that we'll do our very best to get Abe's project in on schedule. I'm just trying to prepare you for the reality that sometimes weather or circumstance keep us from delivering on time. And we'll prepare Abe for the same possibility, okay?"

I was still stuck on the fact that Chance had used the L word, and I nodded my head dumbly, following Chance's broad-shouldered form from the truck and into the office. Where the scent of black licorice pervaded.

My giddy smile faded when I found Sam standing next to my desk talking to my father, who wore a very grave expression. Something was wrong.

"Thought you were sick, little bro?" Chance said, stopping to address the men as I lingered in the doorway.

"Not anymore." Sam's face was almost as serious as my father's. "Park Service needs our help."

"The fire's jumped the canyon." My dad's voice was low and full of worry, and my own stomach twisted into a knot of anxiety in response.

Chapter 12

SAM

Leaving Miranda alone with Chance wasn't what I wanted to do, and as I turned and walked out of the office that morning, every step away seemed to grow more difficult. But the right thing wasn't always the easy thing, right? And when you cared about someone, you did what was good for them—right for them—even when it wasn't what you wanted. Who knew what I wanted, anyway? I'd had a ridiculous crush on Miranda George since I'd been a little kid. There'd been something about her back then, a bright optimistic innocence that drew me in. It was something she still carried, though I felt like now she tried to hide it sometimes, like she'd gotten the idea it wasn't mature to be so open to the world, so eager. If I could figure out who had made her think that, I'd throttle them. Hell, it was probably my brother.

"Hey Sam," Maddie greeted me as I went into the diner. I should've gone home. I'd told Chance and Miranda I was sick, and now that I'd given her time to be alone with my brother, I did actually feel a little sick, but I thought there was a chance Frank's pecan pie might solve the problem.

"Hey Maddie." I took a spot at the counter and sank back

into the cushy red vinyl seat. "I'll take a piece of pecan pie when you have a minute."

"I thought you had that pecan pie look about you," Maddie said, giving me an understanding smile as she pulled a plate from behind the counter and removed the pie dome. "What's wrong?"

I shook my head. Miranda and Maddie were friends, and anything I said here could get back to Miranda. "Nah, I'm okay."

Maddie set the pie in front of me with a cup of coffee, and added a squirt of whipped cream to both. I couldn't help my sweet tooth. Licorice, whipped cream and Miranda George were things I just liked. I couldn't necessarily explain why. But Maddie seemed to understand, at least about the whipped cream. I stirred the cream into my coffee and watched the colors meld and blend, wishing things were just a little bit easier.

For a few minutes, I was on my own, and while the pie and coffee were good, they didn't do much for the strange ache inside me.

"This is not the face of a guy who just needed a piece of pie," Maddie said, taking the stool next to me.

I shrugged. She was right, and maybe I did need to talk to someone. "No, you're right."

"Need an ear?"

I sighed and leaned back, crossing my arms. "I don't know, Maddie. It's not one thing, it's nothing simple."

She squinted and pressed her lips together, and then started tentatively. "Can I take a guess?"

"Sure."

"Is it Miranda?"

A single laugh escaped my lips, but it held no mirth. It was more a sound of relief, in a way, to let that little bit of truth out. "Partly, yeah."

Maddie sat back, clearly waiting for more.

"She likes my brother." Maddie's eyes confirmed that she already knew that. "So I offered to help her get his attention, maybe catch his eye romantically." I dropped my gaze to the bite of pie left on my plate and pushed the plate away. Pie didn't sound good at all now. "So I gave her a couple tips and pretended to be sick, and left them at the office together alone."

"Oh," Maddie said, understanding clearing her features.

"Why do you say it like that?" I didn't know why I was challenging her. It was obvious she could see beyond my words, but I needed to hear someone say it out loud, since I couldn't manage it.

"Maybe you'd rather have time alone with her? Maybe you think she's interested in the wrong Palmer brother?"

I swung my legs to face Maddie, not wanting anyone else to overhear, a concern probably left over from school days when anyone with a bit of juicy gossip like this might ruin your life with it. "I don't know," I said miserably. "It doesn't matter how I feel because she completely hates me. She always has."

"And you've always …"

"Yeah." The years unspooled in my mind. I had no idea how long I'd been fond of Miranda. "I used to just like her, you know? We played together as kids—she was kind of like the little sister I never had. But then we got older …" I trailed off, thinking of a day in eighth grade when I'd felt a bolt of jealousy spear me as I watched Klein Boldt kiss Miranda in the hallway at school. That hadn't lasted long, but I'd suffered through every second of it. Thankfully, Miranda didn't seem to date much. It would have killed me. "It's stupid. Like I said, she seriously hates me. And she likes my brother." Because he was Chance. Because he was perfect. Because no one but me could see past his shiny exterior.

"She thinks she likes Chance," Maddie said slowly.

"She's had a lot of years to figure it out," I assured her.

"But she's looking at the wrong brother."

"Not if you ask her."

"So how do we make her look at you?" I could almost hear the wheels turning in Maddie's brain.

I stood up. "It's okay, Mads. This isn't for you to fix. I appreciate you listening, but seriously. It's fine. It's nothing new. I just need to forget about the whole thing and move on. I've actually been looking at taking over the office down in Fresno, maybe get a new perspective in a bigger place."

Maddie nodded, but her eyes widened in surprise.

"There's not much for me up here," I continued, wishing my mouth would just shut. "I've been here forever, and that was never really the plan."

"Sure," Maddie said. "I get it. But what if—"

I smiled at her, and I could feel the resignation showing on my face. "I've 'what-if'd' it all to death," I told her. "It makes the most sense for me to get my feet on the ground somewhere else. Where maybe I'm the only Palmer brother around for a few miles."

She tilted her head to the side and pulled me into a hug, and even though I would never have reached out to hug her, it felt nice to believe that someone understood, even just a little bit. "You're a good guy, Sam."

"You're not going to say anything to Miranda, right?" I stepped back.

"Of course I won't," she promised.

"Good. Thanks." I turned and moved toward the door. Adele stood at the podium, and gave me a smile that looked like it might have pained her. Then she barked at Maddie. "Back to work, Princess." That was Adele's way of telling us she cared about us. She had a rock-hard exterior, but she was soft on the inside. Maybe. Or maybe she really was just kind of mean, but I'd known her long enough to believe her bark was much worse than her bite. "See you later, Adele."

"Palmer."

I went back to the truck and climbed in, still not excited about the idea of going home. Instead, I drove out to the site of a refurbishment we had going on for the Lesters around the side of the meadow in the village. The old two-story structure was rotting, and we were rebuilding the thing in place, adding a new roof and upgrading the bathroom. Cameron, Maddie's brother, was leading the crew out there. He'd worked for my dad when we were all in high school for a couple summers, and now he threw himself into work like no one I'd ever seen.

I got out of the truck as the wind rose, making a rushing sound through the tops of the huge trees that stood on either side of the road, and something in the air pulled at my senses, though I couldn't say exactly what it was. The sky had been clear and brilliant blue moments before, but now a cloud bank was rolling over us with the wind, and my gut churned for no reason I could identify. I shoved the feeling aside and strode onto the site, where Cam and Jack were up on the roof. I waited until they were both looking up to call to them, not wanting to startle anyone into falling. "Hey Cam!"

Cameron gazed down at me and lifted a hand. "What's up, Sam?"

"Just checking in. Progress looks good out here. All going okay?"

The older man's gaze left my face and he lifted his eyes to the clouds coming in, and the feeling of dread I'd had a moment before returned. "Get down," Cameron said to the other man in a stern tone.

"It's cool," I called back. I didn't mean to interrupt the job, and didn't really need to talk to Cam. As they descended ladders on opposing sides of the cabin, realization hit me, as it had surely hit Cameron just a moment before. The clouds boiling over the treetops weren't clouds at all. Ash began to fall around us, littering the sky like charred snowflakes. Smoke.

"The wind shifted," Cam said, hitting the ground. "Fire's changing directions."

"Better head to the station." I slid into the truck and the two men got into a second truck behind me. We drove to the ranger station in town and parked. Mr. George was on the phone at the desk inside when we entered. We waited until he'd hung up, his voice low as he said, "I understand. We'll do all we can up here."

"Ash is falling in the village," I said. "Wind shifted."

"The fire's crossed the canyon," he said, his face etched with worry. "It's coming this way."

We stood still for a moment, each man letting his own thoughts unwind for a brief time before we took action. Then Mr. George stood. "Sam, I think we're gonna need some help."

"Yes, sir." Together, we turned and exited the station, heading for the office. Cameron and Jack waited outside.

Chapter 13
MIRANDA

"What does this mean, Dad?" Fear began to coil tightly in my chest, and I swallowed hard, trying to push it down.

My father shook his head, his face still grim. "If the fire holds its course, it means we'll be evacuating in a few days. Until then, we need to do everything we can to get a clear perimeter around any structures and give the firefighters the best possible chance to protect the village."

"Shit," Chance said, rubbing a hand across the back of his neck. I could see stress and tension in the set of his shoulders, and I instinctively stepped closer to him, wishing I could help somehow. He dropped his big hands to the surface of my desk and looked down, seeming to think.

"We can take the dozers out behind the ridge down the fire road if the firefighters could use them," Sam said. "Help clear everything we can off the eastern hillsides."

"That'd sure be a help if you guys can spare the men and equipment. The Hotshots are back there, but with so many fires burning around the state, they're short handed." I knew that Hotshots were the experienced backcountry firefighters who did their best to keep wildfires under control. They were like the special forces of firefighters.

"A lot of our guys are down in the valley this week," Chance said.

"I could get a couple men from the village if you could show them what to do," Dad said.

"Miranda, can you take a quick inventory of the equipment we've got up here right now?" Sam asked me. I dropped into my chair and pulled up the spreadsheet we'd been working with.

Within fifteen minutes, Sam had gone back out with my dad to get some volunteers from town, and Chance and I were left alone in the office. There was an unsettled air around us, a tension that hadn't been there before.

"Shit," Chance said, his eyes wider than normal. "This could ruin everything—we've got projects in various stages of completion all over this mountain. Money sunk that we'll never recoup."

I nodded, but I couldn't stop thinking about my own house, about my parents, about what life might be like if we lost everything.

"I'm sorry, Miranda," Chance said suddenly, his face clearing as he looked at me. "I know it's not just me. The people up here ... your family ... no one wants to contemplate losing their house. Do you need to go home?"

I shook my head. "I might just give my mom a call though, see how she's doing?"

Chance stepped toward me and dropped a hand on my shoulder. I was certain it was meant to be comforting, but it was so distracting I could barely think. That was the second time today he'd touched me suddenly, and my stomach flipped upside down. "Of course. Want to use Sam's office?"

I nodded and stood, feeling lost when Chance's hand slipped from my shoulder. "Okay, yeah." I tripped as I rounded the desk, catching the edge of it with my hand and shooting Chance an embarrassed grin. Luckily, he'd already turned back to his own office.

Sam's office was surprisingly neat. His desk was tidy, pens all standing at attention in a little cup and Post-Its next to the phone. His drafting table had several sheets on it, and there were rolls of plans stacked in cubes next to it. I glanced at the drawing on top, and couldn't help but be impressed by the strong clear lines, the way the house he'd drawn seemed to come to life on the page. I was just learning drafting myself, and this seemed so far beyond what I was currently capable of. I'd never really considered that Sam and I had similar interests —designing spaces. His interest was more focused on the outside while I was interested in the interiors. I lifted the top sheet and gazed at the next draft on the table, the landscape he'd hidden from me when I'd walked in on him working before, which was equally impressive. I pulled up a third sheet, unable to stop my interest from leading me to snoop where I probably shouldn't, but what waited there on the bottom sheet of paper stopped me cold.

There, staring out at me with familiar wide eyes, was my own face. I sucked in a harsh breath, surprise flooding me at seeing myself here, in Sam's office, rendered with such care and detail. The drawing was good—it was beyond good, actually. As I considered my own face, I realized two things. For one thing, Sam wasn't just a drafter; he was an artist. I wondered why he kept it hidden. And secondly, when Sam drew me ... I was beautiful.

Conflicting emotions rose inside me. Once the shock had worn off, confusion began to bubble in my veins. How should I feel about this? How strange it was to think of Sam standing in here and focusing like this on every little detail of my face, my hair. I was flattered. Sam was clearly talented. I was honored that he'd use that talent to render my image, but it was still strange. Why would he focus on me this way? As far as I knew, Sam's concern for me was limited to figuring out ways to make me miserable, or at least to embarrass me. His offer to help me catch Chance's eye had been totally out of character and I still didn't know what to make of it any more than I knew what to make of this incredible portrait.

My own face stared at me knowingly, and I dropped the other sheets back over it. I had no idea how to feel about what I'd found, and guilt surged through me. I shouldn't have been snooping in the first place. I didn't know why Sam would draw me, but it wasn't my business, and it didn't change anything. He was probably just practicing. Or maybe he'd use this to throw darts at later. He probably drew everyone in town.

I moved over to the phone and called my house, my brain spinning.

"Hello?"

"Mom," I said, her familiar voice washing some of the turmoil from my mind. "How are you?"

"Well, your father just called. He said the fire—"

"I just spoke to him," I told her. "I wanted to be sure you were okay."

"I've got the fire box in the car just in case," she said. We'd kept all of our family papers in a fireproof box for as long as I could remember.

"Good," I said. "I think we've got time, so maybe we should grab as much other stuff as we can? Photos? Grandma's quilt?"

"Right. I've been making a list." Mom loved lists. "And I called your Aunt Steele to let her know we might be coming to stay for a bit." Aunt Steele was Mom's sister, who lived in Petaluma.

"You've got it all organized." Hearing my mom so put together made me proud. I could never predict any more when she might fall apart and when she'd master a situation completely, but I should have known that Mom would be reliable in a time of real trouble. "I'll be home in a bit, okay? Just going to help Chance organize stuff here first."

"He's lucky to have you."

I sighed. If only.

Sam was back in the office before long, and ten men stood out on the sidewalk in front of the building. "I've got as many guys as we could find," he said, calling into Chance's office. "You ready to head out?"

I followed Chance and Sam outside where they got the bobcats and dozers ready to haul around the fire road to help clear the debris on the hillsides. Men piled into the truck cabs, and I recognized Mr. Adams from the Village, along with John Trench and Maddie's brother Cameron. Dean and Frank must've come over from the diner, and they jumped into the cab of a truck beside Sam. Jack Stiles and Connor and even Mr. Allen had come to help.

As I watched all these local men pull together and set out to try to save our community, something in my heart twinged. This place, these old trees and the tiny little impermanent buildings beneath them, they were our tiny piece of the world and it was touching to see how much the men who lived here were willing to do to save it. Engines rumbled to life and before long the Palmer parking lot was a riot of gravel crunching and gears grinding, and I stepped back onto the pavement next to the backdoor of the building, feeling a little lost. Chance waved from the wheel of one of the trucks, and then pulled out of the parking lot. I wasn't quite sure what I was supposed to do alone at Palmer. I hadn't been working here long enough to have a lot of self-directed tasking.

The last truck began to move, and then ground to a stop in

front of where I stood. Sam slid down from the lofty cab and walked around from the driver's side.

"You gonna be okay here for a bit, Miranda?" His blue gray eyes were dark, concerned, and his tone was soft and careful.

My discovery of the drawing still pulled at me, made me unsure what kind of ground I stood on here with the younger Palmer brother. I was so used to not trusting him, but now I felt like I carried some secret of his—one I didn't understand. "I guess so," I shrugged.

"We'll be out a few hours," Sam said, glancing at the line of big trucks moving out of the parking lot and onto the highway, heading north. "We'll do what we can and then head back. Can you be the operations center here? I can call you from the truck radio. Maybe you can keep the ranger station informed of our progress, and let us know if anything happens?"

"I can do that," I assured him, glad to have some direction.

Sam's eyes stayed locked on mine for a minute, and I wasn't sure why, but the tension made me a little dizzy and I couldn't figure out what to do with my hands suddenly, so I shoved them into my back pockets. "I'm glad you're here," Sam said quietly.

I scrunched up my face and gave him a questioning look. "I live here. Where else would I be?"

"I meant at Palmer," he said. "With me."

"Oh." It was debatable whether I was at Palmer to be with Sam, but whatever softness had found its way into his voice, into the air between us, was something I didn't want to contradict, and something inside me even reached toward it, using it for warmth and comfort in the midst of a scary situation, so I went with it. Even Sam knew that if I was at Palmer to be with anyone, it was Chance. But it was still nice to hear that someone was glad I was here. "Okay," I said, beginning to feel uncomfortable under Sam's intense gaze. He seemed to be trying to decide something, figure something out, and then he took a step back and grinned, and the moment broke.

"Right. I'll be in touch. You have the conn."

"I have the what?"

"Yeah, the control. Of the ship. It's from *Star Trek*."

"So there's no way I'd know what you're talking about."

Sam lifted a shoulder. "Nothing new there."

And he was back. The Sam who wanted to make fun of me and point out how little I knew. I turned and went inside, a strange mix of feelings swirling inside me as I listened to the sound of the huge truck move past the building and out onto the road.

As I sat at my desk stress-eating chocolate-covered raisins, a million thoughts and memories swirled through my mind. The morning I'd spent with Chance and the tension that came with worrying about fire consuming my childhood home must've launched me into a contemplative mood, because suddenly I was sorting through a host of memories from the years I'd spent here. The weird thing was how often Sam popped up in those memories, even when I was searching them for a glimpse of Chance. If there was one thing I could say about Sam Palmer, it was that he'd always been there.

Chapter 14
MIRANDA

It was dark when the trucks rumbled back into the parking lot behind Palmer, and I stepped out to watch them move back into neat lines across the gravel expanse. The men tumbled from the cabs of the trucks, faces smeared with dirt and serious expressions. As they stood in a loose group in front of me, I thought I could smell the woodsy char of smoke, but it might have just been my imagination.

"How did it go?" I asked Sam when he'd thanked the men and walked toward me. Chance stayed with the small group wandering off toward the diner.

"We did a lot," Sam said, and I could hear the exhaustion in his voice. "The hills are so steep the bobcats weren't a huge help for a lot of it. We had guys up there just pulling branches and stuff down the hill with shovels and their hands until the machinery could get to it."

I'd hiked the ridge, and knew the terrain above the old fire road. It was dense and covered with decades of debris. There'd been so much controversy about controlled burns in recent years that the forest service hadn't cleared spaces around the park like they used to, and the accumulated branches, pine cones and needles that covered the ground were basically kindling for any sparks that found them. I cringed as I considered how vulnerable we were up here.

Sam and I went back into the building, and he settled into the leather chair in the front office, rubbing one hand over his jaw. I wasn't sure what to do, or if I was done for the day, so I sat back down at my desk. After a minute, Sam got up again and went into Chance's office, returning with two bottles in his hand. "Have a beer with me?"

I accepted the bottle, watching Sam carefully as he dropped back into the chair. When he was around, I'd always felt a need to be on my guard, to protect myself. But right now, there was something about him that seemed vulnerable and exposed. I almost felt like I should be comforting him somehow. Instead, I just held the cool bottle between my hands and said nothing.

Sam took a long pull from the beer in his hands and leaned back in the chair, his gaze locked on something only he could see, out in the distance beyond the walls of the room. "You ever think about what a weird place this is, Miranda? How different it must have been to have grown up somewhere else? In a big city or something?"

I lifted a shoulder and swiveled in my chair. "Sometimes."

"Like in the movies we used to watch about high school kids, right? Big schools with football teams and cheerleaders …" he trailed off. Our school had none of those things. Our graduating class had been just over fifty kids. "I used to think about what we were missing," Sam continued. "I used to want all that, to be in a place with more people, more opportunity, more … everything."

"And you don't now?" I asked.

Sam's eyes found mine for a moment, and then he looked away again. "I don't know."

I was sweating, but I couldn't have explained why. I hadn't

noticed it before Sam had given me that look. Why did he mess with me like this? I let out an exasperated sigh.

"Sorry," he said, taking my sigh for a sign of impatience. "It just makes you think, you know? Working all day to try to save a place I've wished my whole life to escape. It made me think about what we'd be saving ... or losing. The people here, the quaint little town, the way everyone knows everything about everyone else ... I don't think it'd be like that in most other places. It'd be a shame to lose it all."

That was an understatement. "I can't imagine losing it all ... my parents ..." I squeezed my eyes shut. Sam's family was gone. He might be fond of the people here, the buildings. But if his house burned down, he'd just go somewhere else. My family was still here, my parents were a part of these mountains. I couldn't imagine them in a city.

"I know." Sam's voice was softer. "I hope they can stop it."

I took a sip of the beer Sam had given me, and couldn't help wrinkling my nose as the cold liquid slid across my tongue. It wasn't bad though, and I took another sip. "Do you think you'll stay here?" I'd never really talked to Sam about his plans, had always just taken for granted that he'd be here, at Palmer. "I mean, if things burn down?"

"I wasn't planning to stay either way," Sam said, and surprise flooded me, making me shiver unexpectedly.

"Really?" I asked.

He smiled, but there was no glee in the expression, it was a sad smile. "There's not much for me up here," he said. "And I'd like to meet someone one day, have a family."

That made me smile. "I could actually see you being a really good dad," I said.

He squinted at me. "You say that like it surprises you."

"Just never thought about you that way before."

Something dark passed through Sam's eyes and he dropped my gaze as he said in a low voice, "I know."

"What would you do if you left here?" I was curious, but I also felt like maybe if someone braver told me their plans, it could help me make my own. "Where would you go?"

"I don't know," Sam said, catching my eye again. "Maybe down to Fresno to run things at the office there, maybe out toward the Pacific. I guess wherever I could find work, or convince Chance to set up a Palmer office."

"So you'd stay in construction?"

"That's the gig, I guess. I don't know much else."

I nodded, thinking about how little I'd explored the state I'd grown up in. I couldn't picture myself living anywhere but on the side of a mountain. I might have dreamed about it for years, but now that my home was being threatened, I couldn't imagine leaving.

"Did you get any updates from your dad?" Sam asked.

"Not really. He called over just before you guys came back in. He said nothing had really changed. They've got part of it contained, but the leading edge is still coming this way."

Sam nodded. "We'll move most of the equipment down to the lot in Fresno over the next couple days," he said. His voice sounded hollow.

"Anything you need me to do to help?"

"There'll be some calls to make—letting people know our plans for now, rescheduling. Or just halting work until the threat passes."

I nodded and took another sip of the beer. My skin felt a little tingly and my head felt lighter. Something about the feeling seemed right after the stress of the afternoon.

"You don't have to stay," Sam said. "If you need to get going, or if you wanted to head over to the diner. With Chance."

I'd tried to catch Chance's eye as he'd dropped down from the cab of one of the trucks when the men had come back. He'd been all long legs and broad shoulders, smeared with the dirt of the mountains and looking every bit the hero. But he hadn't even looked my way, had just clapped another man on the back and headed across the parking lot. I shrugged. "Nothing's ever going to happen between me and Chance. I might as well admit it."

Sam shifted his weight slowly forward in the chair, pressing his lips into a line and seeming to think. "Might take some time," he said.

"He's known me my whole life." How much more time could he need? "He's just not interested in me." Something about the darkness outside and the quiet bubble here in the little office had me revealing more to Sam than I normally would. He wasn't exactly my favorite confidante.

"He's an idiot." Sam's voice was bitter. I was used to Sam and Chance picking on each other, and when Sam said things like that, I usually chalked it up to jealousy or sour grapes. But when he said this, it sounded like something else.

"It's fine," I said. "I'm a small town girl. I never really thought I had a shot with him … I just …" I trailed off.

"I know," Sam said, and I wondered what he knew.

"If you agree, why did you say you'd help me?"

He cocked his head to the side and a lock of dark brown hair fell across his eyes. "What? No, I don't agree. I said 'I know' because I know you think of yourself as less than you are. I don't like the way you undervalue yourself, Miranda. And I said I'd help you because …" It was Sam's turn to trail off. "I just want to see you happy."

My mouth might have dropped open slightly. "Really." It wasn't a question. I was so used to Sam having some kind of angle, or looking for the joke in things, that I wasn't sure how to react to the nicest thing he'd ever said to me.

"I guess it's my fault you don't think I'd want to do something nice for you. I've always been—"

"Sort of a jerk."

"I was going to say kind of oblivious." He smiled. "Jerk works too, I guess."

"Sorry," I said quickly.

He laughed lightly and his eyes crinkled at the corners. I wondered why I'd never noticed how handsome he was when he smiled like that, or how nice his voice was, all deep and low with an edge of humor always waiting there. "Maybe I've always been kind of a jerk to you because—"

"Hey guys." The door swung open, hitting the office wall as Chance stepped inside. "Burning the midnight oil?"

I looked at my watch. It was after eight o'clock, and I knew my mother would be worried. "Oh wow, it's gotten late. I'd better get home." I stood and gathered my things. For some reason I was finding it difficult to look at either Palmer brother as I pulled my purse onto my shoulder and dug for my car keys. "See you guys tomorrow," I said, moving toward the door.

"Good night," Sam and Chance said at once, and I stepped out into the darkening night. The smell of smoke filled the air and my eyes teared up, but I wasn't sure if the smoke was to blame.

Chapter 15
SAM

Chance stood in the middle of the office, having no idea what he'd just interrupted. I stared at him as he stood there in all his oblivious glory, his perfect champion good looks shining as usual. He raised an eyebrow at me and chuckled. "What's got up your butt? You should've come to the diner and had a few beers with us."

I raised the beer I still held in my hand. "Had one here."

"With George, huh?"

"With Miranda."

An irritating knowing look flashed across Chance's face and he dropped into the chair beside me. "Thinking of bagging the help?" He bumped my shoulder with his own and I had to work hard to keep from decking him. The problem was that he'd win in a fight. Chance always won. Everything.

"Miranda's not 'the help,' asshole. You've known her your whole life. She's smart and sweet, and …" And I'd said way too much.

"And you've been in love with her for as long as either one of us can remember."

The anger and frustration I felt escaped me in a rush, like

I'd been punched in the gut, and I settled back into the hard leather of the seat. "Maybe."

"Do something about it."

"I can't." I was staring at the bottle between my hands, which was easier than looking at my big brother, a guy who had everything I'd ever wanted and didn't even know it or care.

Chance got up and went into his office, and for a minute I thought we were done, but he returned with a beer of his own. "So what's stopping you from telling her how you feel?"

My brother was watching me, and for once his expression was clear, open. I didn't see the competitive nature I was so used to, didn't see him waiting for an opening to show me how he was better. He was just Chance in that moment, and I let my guard down. After all, it had been just my brother and me for a long time now—since Dad had died three years ago, certainly, but really since our mother had died a decade earlier. Chance had looked out for me, and I'd looked after him in some ways. It had only been lately—since he'd come back with his graduate degree—that I'd felt less than bonded to my big brother.

The truth was that I hadn't wanted him to come back, and there was so much guilt and shame bound up in that knowledge I just ended up defaulting to asshole mode instead of trying to figure it out. If Chance wasn't here, at least maybe I'd have had a fighting chance with Miranda. But standing in his shadow? No possibility.

"Why won't you tell her how you feel?" he repeated.

I risked honesty. "I already know the feelings aren't reciprocated."

"Maybe it'll just take her a while to come around," he suggested, eerily echoing my own words to Miranda just a few minutes before.

The echo continued. "She's not coming around. Besides,

she's had her eye on someone else for as long as I've had mine on her."

It was Chance's turn to exhale and sink into the chair. "I know."

What? "You know?" He'd never said a word or let on that he had the slightest idea Miranda had been in love with him for years.

"I keep thinking that if I don't acknowledge it, just treat her as a friend, she'll figure it out and give up."

"Figure what out?"

He looked up at me through narrowed eyes, his mouth pressed into a line as if the words he was considering were hard to release. "I just don't think of her that way."

"Because you're insane." There was no part of me that understood how any man could look at Miranda George and not fall head over heels in love. She was gorgeous, with those big blue eyes and long blond hair, with her perfect little cupid's bow upper lip and upturned nose, and that smooth soft skin. She was smart and funny, and there was something about her that just told you she was good, too.

Maybe it was growing up in such a small town, though it hadn't had the same effect on me or Chance. But Miranda? The very air around her changed, became charged with optimism and positivity. She was light and good, and being near her made other people feel that way. At least it made me feel that way—like there was a chance I could be good, too.

"No. Miranda's gorgeous and sweet. But my heart isn't exactly available, because I'm in love with someone else," he said quietly.

That caught my attention. "Since when? Who?"

He looked at me like he might be about to tell me something, to divulge a truth he'd kept buried. But then he changed his mind. "Nah." He shook his head and the cocky grin slid back into place—Chance's cover for letting anyone see his actual feelings. "Never mind. The point is, you're free and clear to move on George."

"Don't talk about her like that. I don't want to 'move on' her."

He shrugged and sipped his beer.

"What happened?" I tried. "With the person you love?" Chance had never told me much about his personal life, his feelings. He'd gone away to college and grad school and had a whole life away from Kings Grove, one I knew nothing about. And then he'd come back. And it'd been pretty clear he didn't want to be here. Now I realized maybe it was because he'd left something, or someone, behind.

"Just wasn't meant to be, little bro." Chance stood up then and went into his office, clearly ready to end sharing time.

"Good chat, Russ," I said, quoting one of our favorite movies into the empty space he left behind.

He didn't respond. I dropped my empty bottle into the garbage can and stepped out into the night, exhaustion flooding my body even as my mind turned like a hamster in a wheel. The air smelled of smoke and a knot of dread formed inside me. The next few days were probably going to suck.

Chapter 16
MIRANDA

Mom was pacing with worry when I arrived home, and she rushed to me for a hug the second I stepped through the door.

"Hi Mom," I managed, though she seemed to be trying to squeeze me to death. She'd been alone here all day, I knew, with updates trickling in from Dad and the television news showing only the very worst possibilities for our small town. I looked at the coffee table, which was covered with a sheet of butcher paper divided into columns, each holding a list of items with checkboxes next to them. There were Post-It notes stuck to the lists in various places, and every color of the rainbow must've been represented in Mom's tidy hand. Next to the table were Mom's collection of planners, each spread open to various pages with tape flags sticking out in all directions. When Mom was stressed she planned.

"You've been busy," I said.

She fluttered her hands in front of her chest, as if waving away my concerns about her manic planning. "This is bad, Miranda," she said. "But I've got the car all packed up. We're ready to go at a moment's notice. Just need to grab the last few things on the last-minute list I've got right ... over ..." Mom wandered to the coffee table and lifted the huge sheet of paper, and then began scrabbling around on the floor beneath it. "Oh, Glory. What did I do with the last-minute list?"

I watched Mom for a minute, exhaustion overtaking me and making me unable for once, to join her on the floor and help her find whatever she'd lost.

"Aha!" she exclaimed, holding the list over her head. "Last-minute list."

"Good," I said, dropping my purse on the round table in the center of the room where a jigsaw puzzle lay in the same state of half-completion it had been in for months. "The guys cleared a firebreak on the east side of the hill. If it comes over the ridge, they might have a chance of getting it under control from the fire road."

Mom wrung her small hands and went to the kitchen. "I saved you a plate." She pulled a foil-topped plate from the oven and put it on the table. We mostly pretended the puzzle wasn't there at this point, covering it with placemats when we ate.

"Thanks." I took a few bites of meatloaf, but didn't taste anything.

Mom sat next to me and neither of us spoke, but the air around us was thick with our dual worries and cycling fears.

"It'll be okay, Mom," I said. "Either way."

She nodded and stood to turn on the late night news. Dad still hadn't come home, so neither of us had heard much since the men had come back from the ridge.

"The fire has destroyed two structures at this point," the newscaster was saying. "An old hunting cabin long abandoned, and the historic Canyon Ridge Lodge." Mom gasped at this, and my mind immediately went back to the numerous times I'd sat at the ice cream counter at Canyon Ridge, eating sundaes with my grandparents years ago. I hadn't been there since high school, and hadn't thought of the place in years. It was situated down in the bottom of the canyon all by itself on a long stretch of the highway leading north. "The family that owned the Lodge had been evacuated this morning, and while they expressed sadness at the loss of the historic property, they were comforted by the knowledge that everyone had gotten out in time and that they'd had enough warning to save the things they loved. The fire continues to move west and south, and the tiny mountain community of Kings Grove lies directly in its path. If the fire doesn't shift directions, or the firefighters don't get it contained, there could be devastating impacts to this little town in the coming days."

Tears rolled down my mother's cheeks, and I got up to wrap my arms around her shoulders, leaning my head on hers and trying to transfer some hope, though I didn't feel a lot myself. "We'll be okay either way," I said again.

Mom cleared my plate and as the clock inched toward ten p.m., the door opened and my father came in, wrinkled, dusty, and exhausted. He didn't say anything, just shook his head at us, and we understood. We were poised to lose everything. Mom went to him and they stood in the middle of the living room for a long moment, hugging one another. I kissed them each on the cheek and went upstairs to bed.

THE SKY WAS ORANGE the next morning and bits of ash fell from the sky like apocalyptic snowflakes. The air was dry and parched, and the whole village seemed flooded with hopelessness, like a ghost town just waiting to be vacated. I stood on the front steps of the cabin, wishing for a miracle as I prepared myself to go into work.

I pulled into the main parking lot in town to find Adele and Frank standing in front of the diner, locking the doors. "Closed until further notice," Adele said, her voice bitter.

"They've shut down the highway coming up," Frank said. "Except to residents."

That was bad. The fire hadn't shifted during the night then, and was still heading our way.

Frank dropped a big hand on my shoulder and gave me a half-hearted smile. "Thanks for everything you've done here, Miranda."

"Don't do that," I warned him. "I'll be back at work before you know it, and you'll be cursing my clumsiness just like always."

Adele almost smiled at that.

We stood without speaking for a moment, staring up at the eerie sky, and Connor's big white car pulled into the lot before us. Maddie and Connor joined us on the sidewalk.

"Looks pretty bad," Maddie said, looking around. "What do we do?"

"Be ready to head down the hill," Frank said, and Maddie and Connor nodded and pointed to the SUV, which was clearly stuffed to the gills.

Dad had been at work since early that morning, and I excused myself now to visit him at the station next door, hoping maybe there would be some good news I could share, but his face was grave. "Can you ask the Palmers if they'll help get the back ring of structures wrapped?"

"Wrapped?" I had a wild vision of cabins wrapped in Christmas paper as flames overtook them.

"The firefighters wrap them in foil—it can help repel the fire. The forest service is out behind the meadow getting started."

"I'll get some people to help," I promised.

Dad gave me a weary smile and I kissed him on the cheek and left the office, heading back to where the small group still stood on the sidewalk. Craig Pritchard, the grumpy old man who ran the Post Office had joined them and they all looked around themselves helplessly.

"The Forest Service needs some help wrapping cabins behind the meadow," I told them. "I'm going to get the Palmers and head back that way."

Connor nodded and Maddie looked relieved to have something to do.

Adele and Frank were looking at one another and something seemed to pass between them. "I'll get the coffee on," Frank said, moving back to the locked doors of the diner.

"This is no time to be closed," Adele said. "You all are going to be hungry when you're done saving the village." A smile lit her face for a brief second, and I had a glimpse of what Adele might have been like in her youth, happy and maybe even pretty. I wondered, not for the first time, at the way her personal tragedies had changed her, and wished there was some way I could help. She turned and bustled into the diner, and I hugged Maddie and Connor and then turned to go to Palmer Construction. Both trucks were parked outside, so I knew the brothers were already in.

SAM STOOD as I entered the office, coming around his desk and standing in his doorway.

"Hey." His face was serious this morning, and there was no hint of the smirking jerk I was used to being on my guard around. In fact, it felt like something had shifted a little bit between us, like our conversation the night before, the experience of talking to Sam—really sitting down and talking—had cleared some of the ages-old hurt I'd allowed to build a wall between us.

Stranger than Sam's friendly greeting to me was my own reaction to him. My skin warmed and my heart surged just a little bit, and I found I was happy to see him. As much as I had once dreaded running into Sam Palmer, I realized that in the wake of the hurt I seemed to be finally getting past, I took comfort in his constant presence in my life. Moreso now that I saw him every day at work.

It was possible I'd judged Sam unfairly. For years.

"Hey," I returned, feeling oddly conscious of Sam's physicality as his muscular frame filled the doorway of his office, one of his large hands wrapped around the jamb as he leaned into it. His jeans looked good on him as he crossed one ankle casually over the other, and the corded muscles of his arms, exposed by his gray T-shirt, led my mind to wander idly beneath it, imagining for the first time what he might look like without it on. It was an unfamiliar line of thought for me—at least in relation to this particular Palmer brother—and I pushed it away as heat filled my cheeks.

I looked into the other office, where I could see Chance hunched over his keyboard, typing furiously, and I realized that today I'd checked to see if Sam was here before I'd even thought about Chance.

"How are your folks holding up?" Sam asked, from where he leaned in the doorway of his office. Dark circles made his eyes look bruised and they held a haunted look. I wondered if I looked as tired as he did.

"Dad's busy and tired. Mom …" I dropped my eyes and tried to smile. "She'll be okay."

He nodded and took a deep breath. "We need to get the trucks down to the valley today. We've started calling in some folks to drive."

"Good," I said. "But the trucks will have to wait."

"Gotta get 'em out, Miranda," Chance called. "Better than letting 'em burn."

"Of course," I said. "That's not what I meant." I shook my head, irritated for a moment that Chance really seemed to believe I was a moron. "I just talked to my dad. The Forest Service and firefighters are wrapping cabins with foil, and they need help out behind the meadow loop."

Sam's face brightened for a second, and I knew he was relieved to have something productive to do, just as everyone else was in the face of a potentially hopeless situation.

Chance stood and stepped into the doorway. "Good. That's good." He looked uncertain, and I realized I'd never seen him look anything but utterly confident. "We'll send the drivers out to help with that then, and we'll just have to watch it carefully. We can't let the trucks burn, if it comes to it."

"I'd rather save houses," Sam said.

"Hopefully we don't have to choose," I told them. "I'm going to go help."

"I'll come with you," Sam said. "Send the drivers when they check in," he told Chance, and together we went back to the parking lot in front of the diner, and without speaking out loud about it, we both climbed into my little pickup truck.

I guided my tinny little truck out of the main town parking lot and onto the bumpy one-lane roads of the village where Sam and I had both grown up. Having ridden these roads since we were tiny, we both knew when to tense up over a particularly big dip to keep ourselves from bouncing with the car as it jolted around the poorly kept roads. We bounced and swerved, and after a few minutes, Sam turned and looked at me. I could feel his eyes on the side of my face, and even though most of me wanted to turn and look back at him, there was some part of me that was frozen in embarrassment. "What?" I hissed finally, darting my gaze to his and then shooting it back out the front windshield.

"I just ... I guess I'm trying to figure out if I owe you an apology."

"For years of tormenting me? Yeah, you probably do." I was half joking, hoping to get Sam off whatever strange train of thought was leading him to look at me so intently. My stomach jumped and churned, and I wasn't certain if it was from the roads, or from Sam's sudden and intense scrutiny—or maybe his proximity.

He blew out a breath and lifted a hand to rub across the back of his neck as he shook his head. "Deserved that, I guess." His voice was low, almost sad.

"It's fine," I said, suddenly feeling bad about hurting his feelings. He'd been nice to me the last few days. He'd actually argued with Chance to get me the job at Palmer, said complimentary things that had surprised me more than once, and even offered to help me catch Chance's eye. Now that I thought about it, he'd been uncharacteristically nice for a while.

He still smelled a little like licorice, though. The odd thing was, I didn't even mind today.

"No," he said, his voice deep and serious now. "It's not fine. Look, Miranda. I'm sorry if I ever gave you the impression that I didn't like you. Or that I thought you were …"

"Ditzy? Clumsy? Moronic?" I was pushing forward with the relationship I was used to having with Sam—the one where we treated each other like siblings who knew each other too well and didn't get along. Even though I usually hated it, that was what I was used to from him, and whatever was making his voice sound sincere and his eyes darken when he looked at me, whatever was making my blood rush and my cheeks heat, was putting me completely off balance.

"I have never thought you were any of those things." His words were solemn, and I glanced at him as we pulled up across from the lot where five or six men were busy wrapping foil insulation around a small structure. His eyes held mine and something passed between us, something that made my skin feel tight and my insides twist.

"Okay," I said, my voice giving away every bit of confusion I felt at this change in Sam.

"I just ..." Sam spread his big hands on the dashboard in front of him, and we both stared at them for a second. His fingers were long and tapered, his nails neatly kept, and his hands looked strong and capable.

What an odd thing for me to be noticing.

"The thing is," Sam continued, sounding uncertain, "I think you're actually the opposite of all that. You're smart and optimistic, and you've always thought the best of everyone."

He was right, except maybe I hadn't always thought the best of him. Maybe I'd judged him too harshly, let all the embarrassment and humiliation of high school settle into anger. And maybe since he'd been there—since he always seemed to be there—I'd aimed that anger at him.

"I'm not always a good person," I said, thinking that maybe it was me that owed Sam an apology.

He shook his head. "You are, as far as I can tell." He pulled his hands back to his muscled thighs and turned to look at me then, his soulful eyes searching mine. "It's just been hard for me to tell you what I really think of you for so long. I guess I've fallen into a habit pattern, maybe out of fear or a sense of self-defense. I mean, I know you're interested in my brother, so ..." Sam trailed off, his eyes dropping mine, and I found myself leaning forward, wishing he'd finish his thought.

"What do you—?" I began, but my words were cut off by one of the rangers tapping on the driver-side window behind me. I jumped and let out a tiny shriek, and Sam's face broke into a wide smile. Only for once, I realized he wasn't laughing at me exactly. He was just laughing.

"You guys out here to help?" The ranger asked.

"Yes, sir. I'm Ranger George's daughter. He said you guys could maybe use a hand." I told him.

"Happy to have it."

We got out of the car and the ranger introduced us to a few of the people already at work. He directed us to a roll of aluminum wrap and sent us with a staple gun to the next lot over, where we began wrapping a long shingled cabin.

Eventually the other men from the Palmer crews joined us, and soon the drivers who'd volunteered to take the Palmer vehicles to the valley had arrived, too. Armed with ladders, staple guns and lots of the radiant heat-repellant foil, we were soon moving from house to house. Despite the numerous hands available, Sam and I stayed close together and worked as a team, developing a kind of rhythm over the course of the task.

Some kind of peace had evolved between us over the past couple days, and I found that I liked his steady presence at my side. We made a good team. Maybe it was because we'd known each other so long, but we found we didn't have to speak in order to work effectively together. He'd reach for something and I'd hand it to him; I'd turn to ask for something, and he'd be there with it instinctively.

It was comforting, actually, having Sam there with me. If nothing else, he was familiar and comfortable. And at a time when everything I loved was at stake, it was nice to keep that comfort close.

The day passed quickly, the dry heat of the mountain air making our fingertips crack and bleed as ash continued to drift down around us. We stopped frequently to drink from the coolers perched in the back of the Palmer trucks, and to wipe sweat from our faces with sleeves, or stand for a few minutes in the shade of the big evergreen trees that surrounded us.

Toward the end of the day, I sipped from a plastic cup, exhausted as I looked behind me at the road down which we'd moved, now populated with shining foil structures. I didn't know how tin foil could possibly stand up to a raging wildfire, but if it might give people even a chance to keep their homes, I was all for it.

I sat on a stump, resting my forearms on my knees and trying to catch my breath when Sam sat down next to me, sipping from a cup. He didn't say anything, but he leaned into my shoulder for a quick second, a tiny gesture that seemed to say, "look at what we've done," or "you doing all right?" or maybe both things at once. Warmth flooded me at his touch, and I turned and smiled at him, surprised at my own change of heart where he was concerned. The irritation I usually felt around Sam had dissolved, replaced over the course of several long days with a kind of trust that could only be developed between two people who knew each other well.

Sam squinted at me and his mouth opened as if he was about to say something when a distant rumble sent us both to our feet.

"What was that?" I asked in a whisper.

I was answered by another rumble, a deep unsettled shifting in the sky high above us that was accompanied by a bank of low dark clouds moving in from the north.

"Is that …?" We both stared up at the dark mass of storm clouds rolling overhead.

A crash of lightning ripped through the sky, followed by a sudden earth-shaking boom that sent me leaping into Sam's chest. His strong arms went around me. And then the world seemed to still for long seconds as everyone around us gazed into the dark steel sky, which just moments before had been a foreboding shade of purpling orange. As I stared upward, a drop splashed onto my face, hitting me directly between the eyes. An involuntary cry escaped my lips.

Sam looked down at me, a disbelieving smile on his face, and another drop pelted my cheek. All around us, a steady ticking sound began to develop as fat raindrops splatted the dry ground, and within minutes, the sky had opened up and we stood in the midst of an all-out downpour.

"Yes!" Sam cried, pumping a fist into the air, and as

everyone around us cried out in celebration, Sam's arms dropped to my waist and he lifted me off the ground, swinging me in a celebratory circle. I kept my face turned up to the sky as the water poured down, and it wasn't until Sam put me back on my feet that I realized my own arms were around his neck, and that my body was pressed firmly against his chest.

He grinned down at me, and I felt a maniacal smile on my own face as I stared back up at him. Strange thoughts flew through my reeling mind.

I've known Sam almost my whole life. His arms feel so right around me. He really does have the prettiest eyes.

And when he leaned forward ever so slightly, I didn't resist. His full soft lips brushed mine, and I found myself pressing fully against him, my body instinctively searching for more.

The rain poured down around us, washing the village with new hope for potential salvation, and I let myself enjoy kissing the Palmer brother I'd never thought twice about, a vague scent of black licorice filling my senses and a strange new elation filling my heart.

Chapter 17

SAM

I had no idea how it had happened. I didn't plan it. I'd dreamed it for years, for as long as I'd been old enough to consider what Miranda's softness would feel like in contrast to my own body, what it would be like to pull her tightly against me, to hold her near. To breathe her.

To love her.

I'd known Miranda George practically my whole life, and still I felt like being near her was a privilege I hadn't earned yet, like touching her was a prize I had yet to win.

But we'd spent the day together working side by side, both of us focused on a singular goal, a specific and important task. And in the face of life and death, in the face of losing absolutely everything we'd each ever known, all the petty years-old confusion between us fell away. All the grumbling and irritating jockeying for the upper hand became inconsequential, and for once in our lives we were moving in the same direction. It was as if we were stones working our way down a long canyon on the side of a mountain, tumbling and falling, constantly bumping into one another as we each looked for the most direct path, and finally we were both driving straight down on a parallel course, side by side.

When the sky opened up, and the first fat raindrop splattered on Miranda's forehead, the world we knew seemed to trickle away in rivulets of falling rain, washing everything pretentious and irrelevant from us and leaving only what was true.

Miranda.

Me.

Her laughter ringing through the spattering rhythm of the falling rain.

The furious beating of my heart.

Her head thrown back and her mouth open. Her throat exposed as she laughed up at the opening sky.

Wrapping her in my arms in that moment was as natural as taking a breath, and when I spun her around and she threw her arms around my neck, my heart swelled, and I could feel it expand inside my chest.

This.

I could live in this moment for the rest of my life and it would be enough.

But when Miranda slid down to the ground, her body molding to my own and her arms still holding me close, when she stared up into my eyes and moved in, touched her lips to mine—that was perfection.

For that one moment in time, I had everything I'd ever wanted.

And then it was gone.

Chapter 18
MIRANDA

After a long minute, my brain stepped in to take over for my body, which had clearly gotten out of control. I dropped my arms from Sam's neck and pulled my face from his, my mind spinning, trying to make sense of the desire rushing through me.

I stepped back from Sam's embrace, as the village began to gleam, washed clean of months of accumulated dust and glistening with rain.

I ran a hand over my ponytail, awkward discomfort replacing the searing heat I'd felt a moment before, and I turned away to help the others gather the tools lying around and pack them back into truck cabs and cars. Forest Service radios were squawking on the belts of the few rangers guiding our efforts, and the news was encouraging. The storm, which had developed quickly somewhere east of Tahoe, had rolled down the Sierra Nevadas and hung up just over us. Any rain was good rain in California right now, and in a place where the threat of fire was real and terrifying, it was like being touched by the hand of God.

Giddy with hope and exhaustion, those of us who'd been wrapping cabins had hugged each other—or in some cases, kissed—and then climbed back into cars to head back into town and get whatever news might be available.

As I pulled the car keys from my pocket, Sam asked, "Want me to drive?"

I clung to the familiar irritation I found inside me at his words. It was easier than looking at the other feelings his nearness suddenly inspired in me. "Why would I want you to drive?" I made a face at him and we both got into the car. We were soaked, but the air had been so warm before, there was no worry about being cold, and my little truck had definitely been through worse than a couple of soggy passengers. I squeezed the rain out of my hair before I pulled the door shut and draped it over my left shoulder, starting the engine.

"Just trying to be helpful. Thought you might be tired."

I glanced over at Sam, something in his voice was tight and careful now.

"I'm okay." Neither of us had said a word about the strange kiss we'd shared, but my mind kept replaying it. Tension zinged between us, replacing the warm familiarity that had been there before.

We drove back into town through the soaked and darkening village, and I kept poking at the memory of the kiss as if something about it might change upon examination. It had been warm and tender. It had been comforting, and … exciting. Sam's arms around me had felt good—solid and strong. Sexy, even.

Oh, God, what was wrong with me? Kissing Sam Palmer should have been like kissing my brother (if I'd had one). Especially since what I wanted was to be kissing *his* brother. What had made him do it? Why had I responded?

It must have been some kind of reaction to the stress and

relief of the day, shared by two people who'd been through a lot together. That had to be it. Just a reflex like my mother's uncontrollable need to smooth wrinkles from any tablecloth she sees. It was nothing. And I wasn't going to think about it anymore.

"Miranda." As we pulled up in front of the diner where everyone seemed to have wordlessly agreed to regroup, Sam turned to face me.

I glanced at him, but the sincerity and confusion I saw in those eyes didn't match the decision I'd just made. That the kiss was nothing. And if it wasn't nothing, then it was surely a mistake.

"About the kiss—"

It was immature, but I hopped out of the car just as he started speaking and slammed the door before he could possibly expand on that thought. We were not going to talk about it.

"Come on," I urged, as he stepped slowly from the passenger side. "I want to see what my dad has heard."

Rain continued to fall around us, more softly now but still steady. I just hoped it would be enough to give the firefighters an edge on the fire.

I could see my father inside the diner, the group we'd just been with gathered around, listening. We stepped through the doors in time to hear him answering questions.

"So it's not raining in the backcountry?" One of the men asked.

"The storm moved through there," Dad said. "But it rolled through quickly and didn't hang up until it reached us. The good news is that the structures and ground around them are good and wet, and will be even moreso if this rain lasts into the night as they're predicting. The firefighters were able to contain one part of the leading edge, down to the south. But the western edge is still marching forward, and Kings Grove is still in its path."

My heart sank and I fell onto a stool at the counter. Dean Apcott leaned on his forearms on the other side and was watching me thoughtfully. I gave him a weak smile and he stood up straight and returned with a Coke. "You look like you could use this."

"Thanks," I said.

Sam slid onto the stool next to me, and Dean slid a beer in front of him. "And I'm guessing you could use one of these."

"Thanks," Sam said.

Dad stopped behind me on his way out of the diner, dropping both his big hands on my shoulders. "Heard you did some good work out there today, you two."

I shook my head. "Doesn't sound like it'll matter."

"The rain buys us some time, and that's what the guys need to get a handle on this thing. If the winds die down for a day or so behind this storm, maybe we'll still have a shot."

"That's something," Sam said. His voice was hollow and dull, devoid of the laughter I'd heard in it all day as we'd worked. I was saddened at the loss of the sound.

"Get some rest," Dad suggested. "If you're up for it, we could use more help tomorrow. See you at home, pudding."

Sam lifted an eyebrow at my Dad's pet name for me, but it dropped back into place when I scowled at him. "See you later, Daddy."

Neither Sam or I said anything as we sipped our drinks, letting the hum of quiet conversation around us subsume the need for chatter between us. I was afraid he might try to bring up the kiss again, and I definitely didn't want to talk about that. I still couldn't believe I'd let it happen.

Now when I thought about it, I was able to work up a tiny bit of the shock I would have felt a few weeks ago if someone had suggested I kiss Sam Palmer. The weird thing was, I really had to try. And if I was honest, the shock felt a lot like something else. Excitement.

Mom had spent her day cooking and freezing meals, making labels for Tupperware containers full of "Tuna Casserole" and "Lasagna." She turned guiltily from the open freezer when I stumbled in, her hands frantically trying to fit too many square containers into the small space.

"It's a fire, Mom. Not a zombie apocalypse. We're not preppers."

"I need to stay busy," she said, finally managing to shut the freezer door.

"If we have to evacuate, we'll just leave it all."

She shook her head, sending gray curls shaking around her shoulders. "I've got one space in the car left for the cooler, and we can pack all of this in there if we do it just right. I measured the space, and it's almost exactly the same volume as the freezer." She picked up a diagram from the kitchen counter that looked like a complicated Jenga game someone had drawn. I guessed that it showed all the Tupperware fitting into a cooler.

If we were ordered to evacuate, I couldn't imagine taking the time to follow this diagram just to get that last tuna casserole into the car, but I wasn't going to say anything about it now. We all coped the best we could in times of stress. I pulled a box of Raisinets from my stash under the counter and flopped down on the couch.

"What have you heard, Miranda? Did Daddy tell you if the rain helped with the fire?" Mom stood before me, wringing her hands again with worry.

"Sit down, Mom." I sighed, watching my mother settle into

Dad's big recliner, and then told her everything about what had happened today. Well, not absolutely everything.

A strange look came over Mom's face, and she stood back up, and then pulled a pad of paper, a pencil, and a ruler from her desk at the far side of the room and sat back down. "How wide are the sheets of foil, you say?" She had begun sketching a scale picture of our house.

"Mom—" I was beginning to worry about her.

"I'll just figure out the most efficient way for you to wrap our house. It'll help tomorrow when the Forest Service comes around this way."

I just nodded and let Mom do her thing. Once I'd told her everything I knew about the FireZat wrapping we'd been using all day, I excused myself to take a long hot shower and go to bed. I pulled on a pair of comfortable jersey pants and my favorite 49ers jersey and climbed into the steel-framed bed beneath the quilt my grandmother had made for it when I was a kid.

These things around me, these things I'd always taken for granted—they'd been part of my entire life, and they'd been here, in these mountains, for years before I'd arrived. My family had been here since 1925, and I couldn't believe there was a chance this might be the end of it. I pulled the familiar soft old quilt up around my chin despite the heat, and stared at the rafters over my head. Whorls of knots marred the wood between the eaves of the roof, and I could see individual nail heads where my grandfather had pounded them in when he'd expanded the original structure.

This was my home—the only one I'd ever known. And this place, and all the people in it ... I had no idea what I'd do without them.

As I drifted into sleep with the almost foreign sound of rain pelting the roof, the Palmer brothers took their places front and center in my mind. I'd often gone to sleep thinking of blue gray eyes and a perfect smile, but usually the owner of those assets in my mental image was Chance. Tonight Sam stood beside him, and confusion accompanied the usual longing I felt.

What on Earth was happening to me?

Chapter 19

SAM

I watched Miranda's tail lights disappear down the village road and stood in the drizzling rain for a solid ten minutes staring after her.

What the hell had I gone and kissed her for? Now she was doing her very best to avoid even looking at me. The rest of the day had been almost perfect—if you didn't count the threat of an all-consuming wildfire likely to destroy everything I'd ever known along with the homes and lives of everyone I loved. But I wasn't counting that.

Despite the threat of total destruction, the biggest thing on my mind was Miranda. Her bright blue eyes. Her long blond hair. Her self-conscious smile and vivacious laugh. She was like a little slice of perfection I wanted to capture and keep for myself. Like a photo of something beautiful I wanted to be able to look at whenever I felt sad.

But the feeling wasn't mutual.

Was it?

When I'd given in to everything my body was screaming at me to do and kissed her, it had felt right. It hadn't been awkward or forced. Her arms had slid around my neck, the delicious feel of her skin on mine was like a brand seared into my soul. And she'd pressed herself into me and returned the kiss—the memory of it lit my entire body on fire and I had to work hard to keep certain things from responding too enthusiastically as I relived it in my mind. She had been right there. In the same place I was. The same state of mind. I hadn't imagined it. I hadn't forced her to kiss me.

Had I?

I shook my arms, loosening the knots forming in my neck and shoulders and turned slowly back toward the office, where Chance's truck was still parked outside.

"Hey," I called as I entered.

Chance glanced up from his desk and then cocked his head to the side. "What's going on?"

"Oh, you know. Devastating wildfire threatening everything we love. The usual."

"That's not what I mean. You look weird." He stood up from his desk and walked around it, crossing his arms. "Weirder than normal, I mean."

"Ass."

"Quit stalling."

I hated that Chance had always been able to read me. "Just a rough day. Wrapping cabins with that foil that'll probably just make the fire take five minutes longer to destroy them all."

"So optimistic."

"Where were you all day? I thought you'd come out and help."

Chance nodded. "I was on my way, but Mr. George recruited me to take a bobcat back out to help clear some more debris. I'll come out and help tomorrow. I don't know if there's any point."

"Any point?" I stared at him incredulously. "Now who's being optimistic?"

He shook his head. "I don't know. There's so much shit on

those hillsides it kind of seems inevitable that it will burn. If not in this fire, then in the one that comes next year or the year after. Maybe it's time we start looking at plan B. Move Palmer officially to the valley and be done with it."

"Done with Kings Grove?"

He lifted a shoulder. "Let's think about it. Maybe once we take all the equipment down, we just keep it down there. We've got clients down there. Might make more sense to stay there. More business anyway." His voice was thin and I could tell my brother was as tired as I was. Dirt smeared one of his cheeks and his hair was standing practically straight up. And he still looked good, the jerk.

"It'd be weird to leave. We've always been here …" I had no idea why I was saying this now, when this very thing had been on my mind over the past months. Hell, I'd been planning to leave.

"Things change," he said.

That was true, but when I'd thought about leaving before, I'd always believed there'd be something to come back to here. The idea of the Palmer family pulling up stakes for good and moving to the city was hard to wrap my head around. I rubbed a hand over the back of my neck and grabbed the keys to my truck. "Heading home?"

"Yeah, I'll ride with you." Chance locked the office behind us and we drove slowly home through the sprinkling rain. Suddenly, every familiar rock and pothole took on a new meaning to me. Would I be leaving it all behind soon? I pulled up to the old two-story house and saw it as it was for maybe the first time ever. It was old and worn. The shingles were cracked in some spots and the roof could use replacing. The big open deck that spanned the front needed a new coat of stain and the shed out back was leaning dangerously. In the process of updating everyone else's homes, we'd let ours deteriorate. Once

Dad was gone, it just hadn't felt much like something we wanted to preserve, I guessed.

We moved around each other inside, two bachelors way too used to our routines, our quiet lives. Maybe change was exactly what we both needed. How many twenty-five year olds lived with their older brothers, anyway? And I was pretty sure Chance didn't need to be living with his little brother.

I went to bed that night thinking about starting a new life in Fresno and wondering what it might be like. And as hard as I tried to imagine myself happy in a new place, there was one thing that kept pulling me back to Kings Grove, one person without whom I wasn't sure the word "happiness" held much meaning. Miranda.

THE RAIN DIDN'T LAST. By the time we were shoving gear into the truck and heading into the office just after dawn the next morning, the sky was smoky again and the wind was blowing through the treetops, eerie and forlorn.

"Feels like Armageddon," Chance said as we rode through the village. Many of the cabins were deserted. Some were weekend homes anyway, but even those where our neighbors lived year round stood silent and waiting, their occupants having gone elsewhere until the fire had passed. We drove down the line of foil-wrapped structures that would be on the leading edge of the fire if it came over the hillside, and I couldn't help staring at the big stump where Miranda and I had sat the day before, where I'd held her in my arms after so many years of wishing for it. Where I'd finally gotten to kiss the girl of my dreams. And where she'd then stepped away and acted like it had been a huge mistake and refused to even mention it for the rest of the day.

Maybe it had been a mistake. In her eyes at least. Maybe

she'd been caught up in the enthusiasm of the moment—it was raining, for chrissakes—and I'd just been the closest thing to the man she really wanted nearby. It had been a long exhausting couple of days. Maybe she had just needed a hug.

I shook my head, trying to clear it of all the ways Miranda showed me I wasn't what she wanted.

"What's going on in there? I can hear your head ticking." Chance said, glancing at me as he sipped his coffee from the Yeti cup he'd filled at home.

"Just thinking you're probably right. About leaving Kings Grove. Starting somewhere else."

"Amen," he said, reaching across to tap his cup to mine.

We pulled into the office parking lot and I sat in the cab of the truck a few beats longer, staring over the highway at the soaring tops of the grove of Giant Sequoias for which the town was named. Could I really leave this place? What would life be like in a place where the landscape wasn't practically a physical presence in your life? I squeezed my eyes shut, knowing it would be for the best for me to leave Kings Grove.

But first, we needed to try to save it. I took a deep breath and went into the office.

Chapter 20
MIRANDA

I hadn't meant to sleep in, and when my eyes snapped open to find smoke-shrouded sunlight shifting through the curtains, it was like an engine roared to life inside me. I had things I needed to do. What was happening with the fire? I had to go help.

"Mom," I called down the stairs as I stepped out of my bedroom still pulling on my jeans. "Why'd you let me sleep so long?"

Mom didn't answer, but I found her on the couch with a huge box of Christmas ornaments on the table in front of her and the television showing the firefighters working to beat back the approaching fire. "Miranda," my mother said, her voice small and weak.

"What are you doing? It's August."

"I've been meaning to get these sorted forever," she said.

"Right." No use asking more questions. My mother was in defensive organizing mode. "Dad already gone?"

She nodded, and my heart sank a little. It had to be impossible for her, sitting here all day waiting for news.

"You've got the car all packed, right? If we had to go, you'd be totally ready, right?"

"Well no, not really. I need to choose the most special ornaments to take. All of these have sentimental value, honey. I can't just let them go."

I stepped nearer and poked my nose into the box, pulling out two ornaments. One was a wreath I'd made in elementary school—red and green buttons strung together on a cord and tied in a bow. It was cute, but I wasn't sure sentimental was the right word. The other was a delicate glass angel that probably should have been wrapped in bubble wrap; it was a wonder it wasn't broken. "What's this one?"

Mom's face broke into a sad smile and she reached for the angel and patted the couch next to her. "This was your grandmother's," she said, turning the little glass figure in her hands. I noticed that her nails, usually shining with crimson polish, were ragged and torn. I hoped this situation came to an end quickly, if only so my mother could return to her comfortable routines; she was falling apart. "She bought it on her honeymoon when she and your grandfather went to Paris at Christmastime." She pressed it between her palms lovingly and pulled it to her chest. "It's always been one of my favorites."

"Then it should come with us," I told her. "But why don't you finish this up and come down to town? Lot's of folks are gathering at the diner to share news and help where they can, and we've got people going out to wrap structures again today. Come with me."

Mom looked uncertain, her eyes scanning the overstuffed holiday box. And then she pulled her watery blue eyes back to my face. "Okay, yes. I think that would be more useful than sitting here waiting."

I nodded. "I'll make breakfast. You should probably wear some jeans and boots."

"Good. Yes." Mom sprang up and her face cleared a little, focused on a specific task. "I'll be right back."

Twenty minutes later, Mom and I were headed into town. There were lots of cars parked around the parking lot, most of them stuffed to the gills with people's prized possessions. Most of us expected that today the order to evacuate would come.

Inside the diner, Sam was organizing folks into small groups and leaning over a map of the village spread on a table top. I stepped up close to hear what he was saying and he paused for a moment, looking up at me. Our eyes met and I would've sworn I saw him wince, but then he returned to speaking.

"Mr. George asked us to meet the Forest Service working back here," he pointed to the place on the map where we'd been the day before, "and fan out to cover as many structures in this area as possible." He waved at the back section of the village, which included our house. "The fire's still moving, a little slower now thanks to the rain yesterday, but we don't have a lot of time." He hadn't looked at me again, and as he stood up now, his eyes flitted across my face and fell on my mom. A huge smile broke out on his face and a little jolt went through me.

Why hadn't I ever noticed before how crazy handsome he was?

"Mrs. George," he said, and he leaned in and gave my mom a big hug as Chance came striding across the floor of the diner to say hello.

"It's so good to see you again, Mrs. George," Chance said, hugging Mom when Sam let her go.

I'd never envied my mother so much.

She blushed and waved her hands in front of her face. "You boys," she said, laughing self-consciously. "I wanted to come out and see if I could help at all today."

"Absolutely," Sam said, and he swung his eyes to meet

mine. I smiled at him, feeling suddenly awkward, but he looked away without really acknowledging me, and my heart sank. "You and I will head back with John Trench's crew." He indicated Mr. Trench picking up a cup of coffee and a small brown bag from the end of the diner counter where Adele had set up a snack station for the volunteers. "And Miranda and Chance can head to the other side of the village and get going over there with the Allens."

"Oh, well," my mother said. "I know I'm being picky now, but I'd like to stay with Miranda, Sam."

He nodded. "I hate to lose you on my crew, but—"

"We'll both come with you," I said, my mouth moving before my brain had kicked in.

Sam's face clouded, his eyes narrowing and little lines appearing on his brow beneath the light brown lock that always seemed to fall there. "Yeah, okay."

He didn't sound like it was okay at all. He sounded irritated and annoyed, and I realized with a shock that whatever had happened between us yesterday must not have meant anything to him. Maybe what he'd wanted to say after it had happened was that it had been a huge mistake. It must've been just a result of our exhaustion, the turmoil we all felt over the impending danger. It had meant nothing.

Which was good. It had meant nothing to me, either. Right? Yes, I was totally sticking with that. It made a lot more sense than the sudden rush of affection I'd felt on seeing Sam here already working hard to save Kings Grove this morning.

And besides, what was I doing, giving up the opportunity to work with Chance? What if he lost his mind at the end of the day and decided to lay one on me? Maybe that sort of thing ran in the family. I needed to be there for that possibility, didn't I?

"If the call comes to evacuate, family should be together so we don't waste time looking for people," Chance said. "That means you and me together too, little bro."

Sam let out a long breath, and then said, "Fine," and walked over to discuss rearranging groups with Mr. Trench.

Before long, we were piled into one of the big Palmer trucks, heading to the back of the village.

"This is very exciting," my mother whispered, leaning over to me. "Spending our day with these handsome Palmer brothers." She waggled her eyebrows at me, and I knew with certainty that my crush had not gone unnoticed at home, despite my attempts to cover it.

Great. Mom was many things, but subtle was not one of them. And I had no idea which brother she thought I should be interested in, but at this point, I didn't need her pushing me toward either of them. It was going to be a long day, and the fire threatening everything I loved was suddenly just one of my many concerns.

MY MOTHER'S belief that this was all "very exciting" waned shortly after we arrived at the back of the village for a second day, where the mood was much more serious than it had been the day before. The Forest Service firefighters we met were stern and terse, probably as much from exhaustion as from the belief that the evacuation would be called sometime today if the fire didn't change directions or slow down suddenly. Adele and Frank had set up an all-night operation, according to Chance, feeding crews that came in from the fire line.

"The Lodge opened the rooms to firefighters to crash, too," Chance said as we got started working.

My mother nodded at this, and said, "That's the kind of thing small towns are good for. We take care of people."

I knew she was right, but I wanted to point out that small

towns also gave people too much inside knowledge about one another, that they didn't offer opportunities like big cities, and they forced you to remain inside the identity you developed early on, never getting to reinvent yourself as you matured. And I was tired of being the girl who'd tripped, spilled, and stuttered my way through life.

Chance and I worked side by side through the morning, mostly because Sam seemed to be doing his best to stay as far away from me as possible. I'd hoped to find an opportunity to talk to him—I was still embarrassed about the way I'd reacted the day before after he'd kissed me. And that kiss, and the way it had made my knees melt and my insides swirl around, had been about all I could think of since then. I didn't know what I wanted to say to Sam, but I knew I needed to say something. Beyond that, my body was pushing me toward him. It was as if all the girlish fantasies I'd developed for Chance had suddenly dissolved in the reality of that kiss, and were now focused on Sam.

Sam was still Sam—I knew that. There was still the irritating know-it-all laugh, and those eyes that were always watching me, waiting for me to trip or bump into something so he could laugh. But when he'd kissed me, something inside me clicked into place.

I might not have spent years daydreaming about Sam Palmer ... but maybe that was because he was already there. Every time I turned around, Sam was there. He'd been too close to consider, maybe. I'd grown up right next to him, facing the same direction as him. And when you're both looking ahead, you never really notice who's standing right beside you. At least I didn't. But now that he wasn't by my side, I found that I missed him.

Chance had been stapling foil wrap in a vertical line just over my head on a ladder, while I secured it below. Together we were finishing up the last part of one house before moving on to the next. My mother had gone to get a sip of water as Sam carried a ladder to the next lot. He glanced at me as he passed, and our eyes met for a brief second, but as soon as they did, he looked away. I stared after him, still stapling my heart out. Which wasn't the best way to use a staple gun, as it turns out.

"Ready?" Chance was on the ground behind me, folding the ladder.

I'd been working on my knees, and as I went to stand now, something pulled me violently back to the ground. "What the —?" My chin smacked into the padded foil and I went back to my knees, dropping the staple gun to rub my chin.

"Uh, Miranda," Chance had put the ladder down and was by my side, a silent chuckle coming from his mouth as his hands pulled at my shirt. "You got a little crazy with that staple gun here," he said, and I looked to where his hands were working. The edge of my blue T-shirt was fastened to the foil of the house. I'd stapled myself in place, probably when Sam had walked by.

"Wonderful," I said, still rubbing my aching chin.

Chance managed to free me without tearing my shirt, and then he offered me a hand to help me up, that winning smile focused solidly on me. "There you go," he said, pulling me to my feet. His scent floated around me in the dry air, manly and musky and without even a hint of licorice. His dreamy blue grey eyes met mine, and we stood face to face, closer than we'd ever been.

This right here? This was the stuff of my dreams—Chance Palmer, inches from me, holding my hand.

I waited for the butterflies to kick in, but they stayed still. Flightless.

"You okay?" he asked.

"Yup, just another winning Miranda move," I said, dropping his gaze. I realized Chance was still holding my hand, and my gaze shot over to the house next door where Sam stood, watching us, my mother at his side. She was talking to him, but his eyes were fixed on me.

I pulled my hand back and knelt to pick up the staple gun I'd dropped, heat washing through me. I was finding it hard to believe, but it was becoming clear to me that everything I'd ever believed I felt for Chance was suddenly applicable to his brother, my high-school nemesis, Sam.

I followed Chance to the next structure, where my mother was waiting for me with a cup of water.

"Your face is red, pudding."

"Maybe because I just slammed it into the side of a house?" My voice was bitter as I accepted the water and drank, trying to sort through my confusing jumble of feelings.

"Or maybe because you were just chatting with handsome Chance Palmer?"

I darted a gaze around, dreading the possibility that either of the Palmers could have heard her words, but they must've been on the other side of the house. "That's not it," I said, and we carried a large piece of unrolled foil to the back of the house and began fastening it. "A week ago? I would have said yes."

Mom seemed to perk up at this, her spine straightening a bit as she smiled at me. "I knew it! He's very handsome. And successful," she gushed.

Oh dear, I'd accidentally activated the find-a-match-for-Miranda button on my mother. She did this now and then, though I had made it pretty clear a couple years ago that I wasn't very interested in help in this department. Now she was full speed ahead. "You know, he might have literally saved my life that day on Wake Up Kings Grove," she continued. "He was so gallant after the sheet incident, when I ..." Mom trailed off, still unable to discuss the fitted sheet folding disaster.

"I know, Mom. I think that was part of what made me like

him in the first place." That and everything else about him that appealed to a teenaged girl.

"Well, I think he'd be lucky to have you," she went on. "He's been single long enough really. Wouldn't that be so exciting? A mountain marriage! Oh, Miranda, you would have the cutest babies with that boy."

"You're way ahead of yourself, Mom."

"I know," she said, her voice calming a bit. "I can't help it." She stapled as she talked. "The idea of you and Chance being together, getting married." She turned her head and looked at me, her staple gun pausing in the air before her. "I guess I think if you marry someone local, you might actually stay here."

"Even if I wanted to marry Chance Palmer, it wouldn't happen, Mom. Chance has never given me the time of day. If your hopes for my future are pinned on either of the Palmer brothers, you'd better find something new to hope for. There are no Palmers in my future."

My own strange disappointment at Sam's recent coldness colored my voice. I looked up to make sure my mom had gotten the message that this conversation was over, and my heart sank like a stone to see Sam standing just behind her, clearly having heard every word I'd said. My eyes met his and he narrowed his gaze, nodded his head once, and turned on his heel and walked away.

I leaned my head into the side of the house I was working on. I didn't know what might have been happening between Sam and I, but there wasn't going to be anything more happening there now, that was for sure.

"Miranda," Chance's voice came from behind me. "Did you staple yourself again?"

I pulled my head up and looked back at him over my shoulder. "No, I'm okay, Chance. Thanks."

He grinned at me. "Good. Okay, well if there are any more

staple problems, grab John Trench, okay? Sam says the rangers are asking if we can send the bobcats back toward the fire line, and we need to get the rest of the equipment heading down the hill, so we're headed in."

I nodded, a mix of relief and disappointment flooding me. Sam was leaving? I'd hoped maybe we would have a chance to talk today as we worked, though now that he'd heard me declare myself Palmer-free, I didn't know if I'd have the energy to undo and re-explain everything. "Okay," I said.

"See you later, Mrs. George," Chance said. "Doing good work there."

My mother beamed and then turned to me and waggled her eyebrows again.

I shook my head at her and mouthed *Not. Happening.*

I tried not to watch Sam climb into the cab of the truck as he and Chance prepared to leave, but my eyes followed him even when I didn't want them to. He looked stern and determined, and he didn't glance at me once as he folded his long frame into the truck and disappeared.

Chapter 21

MIRANDA

It was almost seven o'clock that evening when Mom and I rode back to the diner with John Trench.

"You ladies did good work out there today." He smiled at us in the back seat. Poor Mom was so tired she'd dropped her head behind her and was snoring softly.

"You too, John," I said. "Thanks for the ride."

He parked and I shook Mom gently awake. "Let's go get some food and check in with Dad," I said.

She looked around groggily and then agreed. "I am hungry."

We got out and went into the diner, where the work crews from all around the village were coming back in, dusty and dirty and exhausted. Dad sat at the counter, a cup of coffee in front of him as he chatted with Connor and Maddie. When he saw Mom and me, he stood and came to put his arms around us. "I hear my girls are being a big help out there," he said. He pulled back, keeping a hand on each of our shoulders. "You doing okay?"

I stared up at the familiar face, lined with worry and etched with the late nights and early mornings he'd been keeping since the fire had begun moving this way. "We are. How are you doing?"

His lips pressed into a thin line, and he seemed to be thinking for a long minute. Then he tilted his chin down at us. "The call to evacuate just came in. I want you girls to go down to Aunt Steele's. I'll call and keep you informed."

Mom, who had been silent up to this point, looking sleepy and worn out, perked up. "Absolutely not."

"Honey, it's a mandatory evacuation."

"We'll go when you do," she said. Her face, usually soft and sweet, and well—maternal—had turned steely with determination.

Dad sighed. "I can't go yet," he said.

Evidently he'd announced the evacuation just before we'd come in, because people were saying goodbye to one another tearfully, and a few families were getting into cars in the parking lot. Dad sank back down onto the stool he'd vacated when we'd arrived and shook his head. "You can stay for now, but not at the house. You'll have to stay here. I need to be able to get to you at a moment's notice, and that back loop is the most likely entry point for the fire."

Mom agreed somewhat violently, her head bobbing and making her curls bounce. "Everything we need is in the car anyway."

I didn't mention the freezer full of meals, but I didn't think even Mom believed those were for evacuation. They had been cooked for one purpose in the days leading up to this—to help preserve Mom's sanity. Dad clearly wasn't enthusiastic about us staying beyond the order to leave, but he didn't seem angry. Maybe he was just too tired to be mad.

Over the next hour or so, the diner began to clear as people said goodbye to one another and began the drive down the mountain to the valley floor. I couldn't imagine how it would feel to leave my home behind, not knowing whether there'd be anything left of it when I returned. What kind of changes would a raging fire wreak on our town? The structures wouldn't stand—I knew that—but I tried to imagine how hard it would be to walk around the little meadow in the aftermath of an inferno like this, stepping through char and ash instead of pine needles and wildflowers. The landscape of my youth, my life really, had been painted in greens mostly, and a lot of dusty brown with bright swaths of color thrown across it. To imagine it in black and grey now was almost impossible, but if the air outside was any indication, it was coming and I'd see the results soon enough.

Ash floated to the ground outside the windows, and the sky, which had been an eerie dusky orange all day, was an ominous foggy gray as evening fell.

Adele and Frank seemed fine with making the diner into a shelter of sorts, and they actually brought a few cots out from the back and a load of pillows and blankets appeared on one table. Frank turned out piles of sausages and french fries, salads and soups, and those of us waiting for news helped ourselves gratefully.

Chance and Sam came in a little while after most people had left as I sat at the counter with my mother eating vegetable soup. My heart jumped as they strode through the door, and so did my soup spoon. I dabbed at the mess.

They stopped to chat with Frank, their tall forms changing the atmosphere inside the diner and charging it with energy, and I couldn't help staring at their broad strong backs, the perfect tousled hair, the muscled and tanned skin extending from the rolled-up sleeves of their work shirts. Sam rubbed a hand across the back of his neck as he stood talking, and I let my eyes linger on his hand, wishing there was a way I could have one more chance, wishing I had reacted better when he'd kissed me. I'd needed time to process everything that had happened, time that we didn't have that day. And now it felt like it might be too late.

I stared at Sam's back, wishing I'd figured everything out sooner—not that I'd figured much out now, but I knew for sure that I'd been wrong about him. For a long time. Or wrong about my own feelings at least. The attention Sam had always paid me hadn't been malicious. He hadn't been looking for ways to humiliate me—at least not since high school, and maybe not even then. Maybe he'd been trying to get my attention, to make me realize I was looking the wrong way as I mooned over his brother. Maybe he knew all that time that he was the Palmer brother I should have been paying attention to.

As if he could feel my eyes on him, Sam turned. He dropped the hand from his neck and fixed me with his blue gray stare, and after a long minute in which I don't think I remembered to breathe, he came toward me. My skin tingled as he approached, like my entire body was suddenly attuned to Sam Palmer. It was a hard thought to accept, but it was true.

"Hey," he said softly, the shield he'd had in place all day finally disappearing.

"Hey," I returned, unable to think of much else to say.

"You aren't evacuating?" he asked, sliding onto the stool next to mine.

I dropped the spoon I'd been holding back into my bowl, realizing too late that I'd splashed my shirt with soup again at some point in the last few minutes. "We'll go soon, probably. Whenever Dad does."

He nodded, his eyes searching mine for something and then flicking past me to my mother. She was absorbed in the newspaper crossword on the counter beside her, and Sam's attention came back to me.

"Are you guys heading down? Did you get all the equipment out?"

Sam dropped an elbow on the counter and leaned into it,

and I could see how tired he was in the lines etched around his eyes, the slump of his strong shoulders. "We're staying for a bit, but yeah, we got most of the stuff heading down. Kept a couple things up here to help out."

"Help out?"

Sam ignored my question, and his teeth worked the corner of his bottom lip as he seemed to think about something. "I need to talk to you about something," he said.

My heart began to gallop, and my head nodded slowly. Yes, we needed to talk. I needed to find a way to explain that I didn't hate black licorice after all, to thank him for being patient, to apologize for all the years I'd been distracted. "Okay." My voice was a breath.

"The office," he began, and my heart juddered to a confused stop. "We're closing up shop up here. As soon as the fire threat is gone," he said. "And I wanted to let you know, since you've been working with us. We're moving operations down to the valley, and we won't need you anymore. We'll send a check for what you've done so far."

The words cut me like a knife. *We won't need you anymore.* "Oh," I managed, confusion muddying my ability to process what Sam had just said.

His handsome face revealed nothing as he watched me, and the big hand that swiped across his stubbled jaw didn't reach out to calm or reassure me. Only his eyes looked like maybe they didn't agree with the words he'd said. "Nothing for us here really, makes more sense to focus on the valley."

I didn't know if he was talking about business or life in general. "Okay," I said. "So you're … moving?"

He shrugged and a sigh escaped his lips. There was something so sad in the set of his shoulders, the resigned tone of his voice. If I'd been braver, I would have put my arms around him, begged him to stay. But I'd never been brave, and understanding men wasn't something I'd mastered.

"Yeah," he said. "Pretty much packed up everything important. We'll grab furniture and stuff later if there's anything left."

It was my turn to nod. I was speechless. I'd taken Sam for granted, definitely. But it had never occurred to me that he would leave. "I'll miss you," I managed.

Sam's eyebrows rose at this statement, and he looked like he might say something as his lips pressed together and his expression shifted.

"There's one more thing," Sam said, and his voice softened a bit. "It's stupid and it probably doesn't matter now, but I want to clear the record."

My head spun. "Okay."

"Just listen, okay?" He took a deep breath, as if this would take strength to say.

I nodded, waiting.

"That night in the shed, at Chance's party."

"Sam, I—" Of all the things we might discuss, this was absolutely not on my list of preferred topics.

"You're listening, remember?" He said, waiting for me to interrupt again. When he was confident I was going to be quiet, he continued. "Sophie Weiland tricked us both. She told you Chance was out there waiting to say goodbye to you."

I felt my eyes widen. I'd never told anyone what had happened.

"She admitted it," Sam explained. "I confronted her because she lied to me to get me out there, too."

"What did she tell you?" I wondered what in the world Sophie could have told Sam to get him to wait in a darkened woodshed as a hopeful freshman at a senior party.

"She told me you were waiting for me." His voice was sad and careful, and I knew this admission had to be hard.

My heart dropped. "Me?" I whispered.

"Sam," Chance called from the doorway.

We both turned to see Chance standing with my father and two of the Forest Service men who had been at the station since the fire began. Sam stood and I followed him, hanging back slightly.

"I told these guys we could get in just ahead of the fire line here and push more of that debris out of the way," Chance said. He was pointing at a map of the village.

One of the other men spoke. "The fire road is still accessible. If we clear back here, there's a chance they can contain this face of the fire and keep it out of the village." He drew an arc where the fire was currently burning.

Sam nodded.

"Things could shift while you're back there," the other man said. "We'd send our guys, but everyone's already in there fighting this thing. I'll go back with you and Ranger George is willing to go, but Judd has to stay up here to manage communications."

I watched from a couple feet away as Sam and Chance exchanged a look with my father and then nodded at the other men. My heart climbed up into my throat as fear clasped me in a steel grip.

My father kissed my cheek and went to kiss my mother, and Sam glanced back at me and paused as the other men headed out the door.

I stepped close to him, near enough to feel the warmth rolling off his body and get a faint whiff of licorice. I wanted to touch him, but something held me back. "Please be careful," I said.

He stared at me a minute longer, and then reached out and tucked a lock of hair behind my ear. He gave me a little half smile before following the other men out toward the ranger station.

"What was that?" Maddie was next to me as soon as Sam was out the door.

My brain was shifting slowly, having just watched my dad and Sam head out the door to go work directly in the path of a blazing inferno. I turned to face her. "What was …?"

"With Sam? Meaningful looks exchanged, and I swear I saw him touch your hair." She smiled at me, lifting her eyebrows in question.

I shook my head, the confusion I felt mingling with the fear and worry and all the tension that had been piling up since the fire began, and even before. "I don't know what that was, really."

Maddie took my arm and steered me back toward the counter, sitting me next to my mom and going around the other side. "Tea?" she asked us, "or …?" She held up a beer bottle.

My mother gave me an odd look, like she wasn't sure she should be drinking in front of me, and then pointed at the beer bottle. "It's been a long day." Her tone was apologetic, and I bumped my shoulder into hers.

"It has," I agreed, my head still spinning. "I'll take one too, actually."

Maddie nodded and then placed two more bottles on the countertop before she leaned on her forearms and fixed me with a direct stare. "Okay. Now spill."

I glanced at my mother, and the fatigue and worry on her face made a little hard place form in my throat. "It's just…" I stared down at the bottle in my hands. "In the middle of what we're all facing here, it's nothing. It's silly to even talk about anything but the fact that everyone we know might lose everything."

Maddie nodded and straightened up, taking a sip of her beer. And then my mother surprised me. She lifted her own bottle to her lips, took a healthy dram, and then looked between me and Maddie. "I don't know what would be better actually, than to be distracted from everything going on around here right now. I, for one, could use it." She took another long pull on the beer and I tried to remember the last time I'd seen my mother drink.

"Okay," I said, not sure how to approach this new side of my mom and equally unsure whether sharing my forlorn-girl drama with my mom was going to be helpful to anyone in any way. "Well," I started. Maddie leaned forward again, a gleam in her dark eyes.

"I've been in love with Chance Palmer my whole life," I said.

"I knew it," my mother crowed. "I think we're all just a teensy bit in love with Chance. Don't tell your father." Mom patted my arm lightly.

"Of course not," I said.

"My lips are sealed," Maddie added.

"Well," my mother said, cocking her head to the side and then turning to look over at Connor Charles typing away on his laptop in the far booth. "Maddie might not be in love with Chance. She's got Connor."

We all took a moment to stare at Maddie's fiancé as he worked. He was pretty glorious, with his determined chiseled jaw and his dark red and gold hair. Sensing our eyes on him, Connor looked up. When he caught us all staring, he made a comical face, scrunching his nose up and shaking his head slightly. We laughed and turned our attention back to the intimate space between us.

"Anyway," I went on, starting to find that I actually wanted to talk about the confusion I'd been feeling. "It's always been Chance. I mean, he's perfect, right? And then there's Sam."

My mother and Maddie both nodded, though I didn't think they had any idea where I was going with this.

"And he's always driven me nuts."

"Really?" Maddie asked, looking surprised. "I knew you liked Chance, but Sam is a good guy."

"I have a hard time deciding which one I like best," Mom said. Her beer was almost empty, and she pointed at it, causing Maddie to run back to the fridge to grab her another.

"Well, you're not alone there," I told her as Maddie returned. My mother's eyebrows shot up, but she didn't say anything else. "Sam was just always around, you know? We were in the same classes, always at the bus stop together. Our high school wasn't exactly huge, so it wasn't like there were a lot of other places for him to be, but it just seemed like every time I turned around, he was there."

"Right," Maddie said, encouraging me to continue.

"So he witnessed a lot of my most humiliating moments." I corrected this. "My *most* humiliating moment, actually."

My mother hiccuped and then rolled her eyes at me. "Can't be worse than showing your bloomers on television."

I laughed at the word 'bloomers'—it was such a Mom thing to say. She meant 'showing your ass' but was way too polite to say it. Maddie gave me a questioning look and I tried to say 'let it go' without actually making a sound. A vivid reminder of my mom's own most humiliating moment, combined with two beers, might leave my mother in tears, and that wasn't the goal. She had enough to worry about with Dad heading back to the fire line.

"I was only seventeen, so it felt pretty horrible," I said.

"Now you have to tell us." Maddie widened her eyes at me, waiting.

I sighed. I might as well. "I showed my boobs to the whole school at prom."

My mother choked on her beer, and Maddie screeched, "What?"

"Not on purpose," I said, glancing around to see if anyone else was listening. My mom stopped coughing, but she still looked horrified. "I tripped going up the stairs, and I guess I caught the hem of my dress and it pulled the whole thing down. Sam was right behind me on the stairs, and I jumped right back up and went onto the stage. I didn't realize my dress was pulled down so low."

"And Sam?"

"I don't think he noticed right away, but then he totally did —mostly because the entire school was screaming in laughter," I cringed as I relived the memory. "And he kind of grabbed me, like pulled me into a hug so his back was to the audience."

"He was trying to cover you," Maddie said, grasping the obvious, something I hadn't been able to do at the time.

"I think so, but at the time, I thought he was making a joke of it somehow, or … I don't know, I was already so embarrassed I couldn't think, and then Sam was hugging me, and my boobs were still out, and it was all so horrible."

My mother's eyes were filling with tears. "You never told me about this," she said quietly.

"What could you have done, Mom?"

"I could have known. It's a Mom's job to know. Just …" she sniffed. "To know the things their kids have to deal with."

Wonderful. I'd managed to make Mom cry even without revisiting Sheetgate.

"Sorry, Mom. I couldn't bring myself to talk about it."

"How'd you get off the stage?" Maddie asked, clearly a little bit fascinated by my horrific high-school humiliation.

"Chance saved me, actually. He was a chaperone, and he put his coat over me and walked me off stage."

"And did you and Sam ever talk about it?" Maddie asked while my mother continued to sniff and look sad.

"No. Definitely not. Between that and the other freshman year humiliation," I said, and my mother's eyebrows shot up to learn there was another defining event in my life she hadn't been aware of. "Sorry Mom," I said, and then I explained about Chance's party and the woodshed. "I guess I just have always felt like Sam's role in my life was to humiliate me."

"But maybe he's just always been too close to see clearly," Maddie said.

I nodded. "Yeah, I think so. Anyway, I'm confused because he kissed me the other day, and now I think I've been chasing the wrong Palmer brother all along."

Both my mother and Maddie gasped. "He kissed you?" Maddie asked, grinning.

"Yes, but I didn't react super well."

"How do you react badly to a kiss?" she asked.

"I think pretending it never happened and refusing to talk about it qualifies," I said.

"Oh, honey." Mom looked ashamed on my behalf, and my heart shriveled even more in acknowledgement of what a moron I was when it came to love. At least she'd quit crying.

"And today he told me they don't need me at Palmer anymore because once the fire is over both he and Chance are moving down to the valley." The last part came out in a rush, and real tears spilled down my cheeks. "And now I'm crying." At least I'd mastered the obvious. I lifted a hand to wipe at my face and accidentally swiped the neck of my beer bottle, sending it toppling over, spilling beer into Mom's lap. "Oh God, I'm a disaster."

We grabbed napkins and cleaned up Mom, the counter, and my face, and then resumed our tight little circle.

"You want to know what I think?" Maddie asked. She didn't wait for either of us to reply. "I think Sam's always had a crush on you. He watches you all the time when they eat in here, you know."

"I always thought that was just so he didn't miss a chance to make fun of me if I spilled something."

"Can't have been easy watching you make google eyes at his brother," Mom said.

I sat up straighter. "I do not make google eyes." What in the world were google eyes, anyway?

"You moon over him." Mom said.

"It's not nineteen-fifty, Mom. People don't moon anymore."

"Whatever. You know what I mean. Poor Sam, watching you watch Chance all those years." She made a dramatic frowning face and I couldn't help but laugh a little bit.

Maddie slapped the counter. "Well it's pretty simple. When he gets back, you tell him how you feel."

"Sure, that's simple." I rolled my eyes at how not simple that was turning out to be. "I've tried to talk to him, but he's avoiding me. And now he's moving away. I think it's just too late."

"It's never too late, Miranda." Maddie looked so optimistic I almost wanted to believe it might be that easy. If nothing else, it was worth a try.

Chapter 22

SAM

Driving headlong into a raging fire seemed like a perfectly rational thing to do after telling the girl you'd always loved that you were giving up on her.

Okay, so maybe I didn't use those exact words. And maybe I'd never actually told Miranda a thing about how I really felt. But I'd always hoped that one day she'd notice. Of course with Chance's shining persona always standing in the way there was little opportunity for that.

"Shit," Chance breathed as we rode with the Forest Service and Mr. George out the back fire road and toward the fire. The sky was glowing the closer we got, and the smoke was thickening around us. When we finally pulled all the way around the village, we could see the blaze roaring less than a half mile away, bulging and spitting like a beast just waiting to rush forward.

"There's a break back there that's holding for now, but the other arm of the fire hasn't been contained and that's what we're worried about. It might come down this way, and if it gets in here past the fire break, it'll run right through the village."

I stared at the part of the fire that the Hotshot crew had contained. It didn't look contained to me, it looked terrifying and ridiculously close. "This is insane," I said. No one disagreed.

We unloaded the bobcats from the back of the flatbed trailer and followed directions. The goal was to push all the debris down to the southern edge of the hillside, out of reach of the oncoming arm of the fire. The firefighters would burn just in front of the advance, hoping to deprive the flames of fuel so there was nothing for it to burn and they might finally be able to stop it. We were just a mile from the back of the village—the line was perilously thin.

Sweat rolled down my face as I struggled to push broken branches and mountains of pine needles and other brush off the hillside and down the southern face. Mr. George and the Forest Service firefighters with us hacked at vines and roots with chainsaws and axes, and Chance and I pushed load after load out of the way with the track loaders. There was a sound —a steady roar—that I realized right away was the fire, and I had a sense of being in the path of an oncoming train. This thing was enormous. How the hell could we stop it by moving some twigs around?

Still, I worked, and hours flew by as we carved a dirt path where brush and ground cover had been heavy before. This was the line, I realized. We were drawing the line that might save everyone and everything we loved. And if it wasn't good enough, or if that roaring beast just ahead was too strong?

We'd lose everything.

And so would everyone we knew.

So would Miranda.

I couldn't stand the images that kept flying through my mind of Miranda and her family sorting through the charred hulk of their home after the fire had burned through. I couldn't let it happen. I might not be able to convince her that we were meant to be together, that I could give her a future—hell, if I was truthful, I'd never actually tried—but I could at least do my best to make sure she kept everything she had now.

Memories of the moments we'd shared in the rain drove me forward. As the heat and horror of the fire seemed to draw nearer hour by hour, I pushed ahead, thinking about how it had felt to finally pull her into my arms. It was like years of longing had flowed out my fingertips, poured from my chest, filled that kiss. And she'd kissed me back. I knew she had, even if she didn't want to admit it. Maybe that was enough—just the knowledge that for a few sweet minutes as the rain poured down around us, Miranda George had kissed me back and held me tight.

Hell, no. That wasn't enough.

"Shit! Over there!" One of the hotshots was running past the bobcat as I pushed another load down the slope, and I looked to see where he was headed just as another sprinted past. I had no idea how they managed to move so quickly when each one of them carried three chainsaws and a mountain of other gear strapped to their bodies. I turned the bobcat and saw what they were running for—a spot of fire had erupted past our break, ignited by embers carried on the wind that rushed above us.

They got the spot extinguished and came back to me a few minutes later, looking every bit as dirty and tired as I felt. "Keep an eye out for those. Drink plenty of water," they advised as they stopped next to the tractor. "Easy to forget, and the heat'll steal your hydration. Last thing we need is one of you guys passing out."

I dutifully lifted my water bottle to my lips and drank.

"I don't know how much more we can do back here," one of them said, looking up. "Weather's supposed to shift soon. The wind'll probably die down when the sun comes up. If we can keep it back till then we might have a shot."

The night stretched out around us, dragging itself forward in shades of orange and red, and casting the men working near the fire in its eerie glow. When we couldn't get the track loaders into a spot or the hill was too steep, Chance and I were on our feet next to Mr. George and the firefighters, working with axes, shovels, and chainsaws to get through the brush and get it out of the fire's way. The gear they'd given us was heavy and hot, and after hours had passed, I began to feel like a zombie, working mindlessly as my brain cranked around Miranda and the idea of leaving Kings Grove. Her face when I'd told her the plan my brother and I had agreed on wasn't exactly thrilled, though I wouldn't have expected her to be. She had looked surprised … and was it wishful thinking to imagine she'd looked sad?

A couple hours before dawn, we'd carved a pretty significant line into the hillside that stretched a good half mile around the back of the village. I was bone tired, and Chance didn't look much better, leaning against the little Bobcat, swigging water and staring out into the crackling glow beyond us.

"Surreal, isn't it?"

"Fucking terrifying is what it is," he said.

I couldn't disagree with that. "I'm almost too tired to be scared now."

Chance looked at me and nodded. "You really going to be okay with everything? Moving? Taking the business down the hill?"

"If the house burns, it'll make the choice easy," I said, not wanting to rehash our decision. I wasn't okay with it, but I didn't have a rational reason not to be. "It makes good sense. For the business, for us personally."

"For us personally," Chance repeated thoughtfully. "You sure about that part?"

"Something you want to ask me?" I was too tired for subtlety.

"Have you told her how you feel yet?"

I shook my head, watched Chance unwrap a stick of gum.

"Maybe you shouldn't leave until you've given yourself a shot with George."

"Don't call her that." I knew Miranda hated being called George. "She hates it."

Chance grinned at me and nodded, handing me a stick of gum.

"How long have you known she had a thing for you?"

"Since high school, for sure."

"And you were seriously never interested? Not even then?" My disbelief colored my words.

"I could have been maybe," he said, his eyes crinkling as he grinned at me. "But you were my brother. And I didn't want to take your girl."

I shook my head at him. He hadn't been oblivious—he'd been standing back for me.

Some shouting had begun off to our side, but it was hard to hear the words because of the ambient roar around us. Chance and I both stared in that direction, trying to make out who was yelling, and why. We stood and started moving toward the sound.

Just then, one of the hotshots came bolting toward us from the direction of the flames. We'd been on the far edge of the line we'd created, farthest away from the fire. Miranda's dad and the other Forest Service workers were closer to the flames, and we hadn't seen any of them in a while. "We got some spotting down here toward the leading edge," he said, his voice tense through his heavy breath. "It got big before we could get it out and came back around. Ranger George is trapped back there."

Shock brought me upright and my bloodstream flooded with adrenaline. "What can we do?"

"Nothing now. Get these tractors loaded up and get out of here. It's too dangerous to have you guys back here at this point. He's in a pocket back there, and we'll get him out. We can't risk having you guys in the line of this thing now. It's moving." He motioned toward the flatbed parked up on the fire road. "Get this equipment out or you might lose it," he said, and began moving back toward the fire.

I couldn't just leave. Not if Miranda's dad was in trouble. What would I tell her? What would I tell her mom?

I helped Chance load up the equipment, and we stood next to the truck for a few minutes, neither of us feeling right about leaving.

Chance seemed to make a decision, and he swung up into the cab of the truck. "I'll drive these out to the lot at the edge of the fire road a mile or so down and park. They'll be safe there. I'll be back."

That's how it had always been with my brother—we'd always been of one mind, followed a similar trajectory of thought. We didn't need to talk about things most of the time because we were almost always on the same page.

"I'm gonna go see if I can help." I turned and began jogging back toward the face of the fire, my muscles screaming with fatigue and my mind still spinning in a thousand directions. The only thing I knew for sure was that I couldn't leave Miranda's dad in danger. As I approached the spot where the hotshots were watering the ground and yelling back and forth to each other, one of them looked up and saw me.

"Told you to go back," he shouted. "But as long as you're here, grab the end of this hose and pull!"

The firefighters had a tender parked close to where we'd come in on the fire road, a big truck full of water with a long hose attached, and they'd been working close to the fire to keep the ground wet and the fire back. Now they were trying to make a hole through the arm that had advanced to get to Mr. George.

I'd been at this end of our firebreak only once all night, when we'd first arrived, but Chance and I had been directed to work back farther, to build the line in case the fire jumped the break the hotshots had been working all day. Mr. George was caught back there somewhere, close to the original line, and I just hoped he was okay. The hotshots seemed to think there was a pretty big pocket, but we all knew eventually the fire would progress to meet itself.

The noise from the fire and the water bombers dropping over the back lines of the fire was incredible, and I had the sense that this would be what the apocalypse looked like—flame and noise and hopeless fear. I held a length of the heavy hose in my gloved hands, and tried to push it forward, feeding it to the fireman who was spraying down the base of the flames, trying to get to Miranda's dad somewhere beyond that fiery wall.

After a while, Chance joined me holding the hose, and I couldn't help feeling useless, just standing there doing almost nothing. I clapped my brother on the shoulder and ran up the length of the hose to the front, where the hotshots had almost managed to douse the line in a spot big enough to see the pocket behind. It was like a fiery portal in some sci-fi movie, flame burning all around the edges and barely simmering on the ground, but it was a portal all the same. And I would have been smarter, I would have been more restrained—if I hadn't gotten a glimpse of Mr. George through the smoke and shimmer of flame, lying in a heap on the ground as the fire threatened to close in around him.

"Mr. George!" Someone yelled, and a minute later, my body was in motion. Heat intensified all around me, and the firemen on the line were shouting in surprise, and I was running directly into the line of flame. I hadn't thought—I was too tired and terrified for that. I'd only reacted, and by the time I got to Mr. George and was kneeling next to his limp form on the ground, it was too late to rethink it. I realized it had been me who screamed out his name.

"Hey," I shouted, rolling him to his back and pulling off a glove to search his neck for a pulse. There was a weak beat in his neck, and relief washed through me. He was undoubtedly suffering from smoke inhalation, and as I watched a hotshot dash through the smoky air toward me, I realized I'd be in the same position soon if we didn't both get out of here.

"Hey," the hotshot yelled at me. "Are you fucking suicidal?" I stared up at him, and realized he was right. I had no business back here. I'd never fought a fire in my life, I'd only known I needed to save Miranda's dad. The man shook his head at me, the serious face streaked with grime and dirt. "Get him up," he shouted.

I did as he said, and we hauled Mr. George between us, prepared to run with him back through the hole in the wall of flames. Only when we turned to go, it had disappeared.

"Shit!" The hotshot yelled. "Shit!"

We dropped Mr. George carefully to the ground and stared at where the hole had been. The raging fire was less than a quarter mile from us on all sides, and it was clear it wouldn't be long before this pocket of cleared ground was overrun. We had nothing to fight it with in here, and the smoke was thick around us. The hotshots had explained earlier that backcountry firefighters didn't use respiratory equipment. They had enough gear to haul, and there wasn't a breather on the market that would work for their needs. When I asked how they managed to keep their breathing clear, they looked at me like I was an idiot, and said they tried to stay out of the smoke. Impossible in here.

"What do we do?" I asked the man, my voice nearly a scream.

"We wait." He pulled a cloth from his pocket and held it over his mouth, dropping to the ground in a crouch. "Get ready to move. The second that hole opens back up. We may not have much time." The hotshot pulled a heat shield blanket from his pack and unfolded it, draping it over Mr. George to block some of the radiant heat from the fire. "You get one of these?" The guy asked me.

I nodded. They'd given me a pack when we'd arrived.

"If the fire's coming and we can't get out, cover yourself with it."

He was serious. If the fire was coming, I was supposed to cover myself with a blanket and hope the fire would just move over me? I knew I'd end up cooked under that blanket, but I just nodded dumbly and cursed the blazing night around me, which felt like it had gone on forever.

We crouched in the thick smoke, surrounded by flame on all sides, Miranda's unconscious father at our feet, and I watched the eerie cast of red dance on the ground before me knowing the shadows moving there were telling the story of how I might die.

If I did manage to survive, I told myself, I wouldn't let another day go by without telling Miranda how I felt.

Chapter 23

MIRANDA

We'd all made up little beds on the cushioned benches in the booths along the walls of the diner. It felt weird to try to sleep in the place I'd worked since junior high school, and as I nestled my head into a borrowed pillow against the back of a booth, I tried not to think about how many different things I'd personally spilled on this exact upholstery. Mom had been given one of the few cots that Adele and Frank had found, and the older couple had finally said goodnight and gone up to their apartment above the diner.

The place had the feeling of a shelter—I guessed that was what it was, really. We were all trying to get a bit of sleep, waiting for news that we knew would probably be bad.

As I thought about everything that could happen in the next twenty-four hours, I couldn't help my mind reaching toward the fire, toward the place where Sam and Chance and my dad were all doing everything they could to help. I hadn't expected them to be gone so long, and I knew my mom was worried, though she was trying to put on a brave face as the hours ticked by. At one point, she'd helped Adele rearrange the under-counter storage, and freed up a pretty big amount of space down there. She really was good at her job. Maybe it was time to go back on the morning show and demonstrate something else so she could redeem herself, or at least regain her self esteem.

Angela Sugar had stopped through the diner earlier in the afternoon—she didn't actually live up here, but kind of pretended to on the morning show. She had a vacation home around the meadow and had come to retrieve things she didn't want to lose in the fire. The show was actually filmed at a studio halfway down the hill. When she'd been in, my mom had run into the back and pretended to be busy back there. When this was all over, I wanted to do something to help my mom regain her confidence. Maybe Angela would be willing to help.

I'd finally begun to drift to sleep when I heard the diner doors open again, and the crackle of a radio. I glanced up to see Ranger Hammond, one of Dad's co-workers at the local station. He looked around, a strange expression on his dark weathered face, and then he spotted my mother asleep on a cot. I pushed myself to sitting and motioned to him just before he leaned down to wake her. He walked over and slid into the bench across from me.

"Miranda, hey."

"What's going on?" I asked him.

He shook his head and took off his hat, dropping it on the table and running a hand over his almost white hair. He wasn't bald, but he kept his tight curls cropped so closely that his hairline almost looked drawn on, the bright hair clear against the dark chocolate of his skin. "I've got some news on the fire," he said, sounding like he wished he could be anywhere else. "Think I should probably talk to your mom."

I shook my head. "She's been a wreck tonight. Can you let her sleep? Tell me instead. I'll wake her up if I need to."

He glanced at my mom again, and her peaceful face must have convinced him I was right. "Okay." His voice was thin and weary. "It's your dad, actually."

Fear crept through me, sinking its teeth into my heart. "Dad?" My voice creaked.

"The fire's advanced a bit in one spot where your dad was working, and he got trapped behind it. In a pocket, like."

I tried to imagine how that could happen, and felt my head shaking slowly back and forth.

"There's a couple other guys back there with him. One of the Palmer brothers and a hotshot, from what I've heard. Trying to find a way to get them all three out now." He didn't look hopeful.

The fear inside me compounded and I felt nauseous. Sam or Chance was trapped too? "Which Palmer brother?" I asked, my voice stronger than I felt.

"Sam, I think. Not completely sure. That wind is pulling the whole thing forward, and the firefighters have their hands full."

Sam. And my father. My heart threatened to stop and I wanted to collapse into a puddle of tears. "What can we do?" I asked, standing as if I could run and help, though I knew I couldn't.

"Wait." Ranger Hammond stood up too, still facing me. He stared down at his feet and then looked back up at me, his features softening. "Some of the guys thought we shouldn't say anything to you or your mom," he said. "But I know what a shock it is to hear bad news, and I thought it would help if you had a little warning about the possibility that …"

"That they won't get out."

His eyes slid to the side and he took a deep breath before saying, "Right."

I sucked in a breath and fought the tears working their way up my throat. "Thanks for telling me, Hal."

"Course." He looked at Mom again. "Think we should wake her?"

I stared at my mother's peaceful face, and imagined how it would change if I told her Dad was trapped by the fire, that he might not come back to us. "No," I said. "I'll tell her when she wakes up. Let her have a few more minutes at least."

Hal dropped a big hand on my shoulder and squeezed, and nodded over my shoulder at someone. I turned to see Maddie standing there, looking worried. "I'm gonna head back, see what other news I can get," he said.

Maddie stepped forward and put her arms around me. "I'll wait with you."

"You heard?"

"Yeah," she said, and we walked together to the booth where I'd been sleeping.

"Think I should wake up my mom?"

Maddie shook her head. "Let her sleep a bit. Maybe they'll be out before she wakes up."

I lifted one side of my mouth in an attempt to smile, but I didn't feel confident they'd be coming back. And the idea of losing my dad...and Sam...it was too much.

MADDIE MADE coffee and we sat in the silence of the sleeping diner for what had to be the longest hours of my life. The world outside the windows turned from an inky black to a smudge of charcoal gray, and finally, as people around us began to stir, a creamsicle orange peeked in through the bottom. We didn't get another update from Hal—or from anyone else—and I felt like worry was eating me from the inside out. There'd be some vague relief in sharing that worry with everyone else, but I knew it wouldn't do anything to solve the actual problem. And I didn't know if my mother could take hours of fear. She was just beginning to wake, and I steeled myself to have to tell her the news.

"I want to tell you it'll be okay," Maddie whispered, staring at the tabletop for a long moment before raising her eyes to meet mine. "But I don't know what to say."

I smiled, but only because I understood. I didn't know what to tell myself, either. "I know. I just find myself sitting here thinking about all the things I never said, all the things I should have said—could have said. Or done."

"Your dad knows how much you love him," she said.

And for a second I was confused. "Of course," I said quickly, ashamed while I was terrified for my father, much of my mind had been focused on Sam, on the idea that I might never get the chance to be honest with him about what I'd only begun to admit to myself. There was something between us. Something beyond childish bickering and constant irritation.

"You meant Sam," she guessed.

"And my dad," I said. "But yeah. Sam. I think I screwed everything up, Maddie. And now it's probably too late … I might never get to tell him."

She shook her head, sending the dark curls bouncing over her shoulders. "Don't do that. We don't know anything yet. All we're doing is waiting."

Waiting. She was right. I needed to wait.

It was only five o'clock, but Good Morning Kings Grove was on, so Adele switched on the television above the counter and set the volume low. Angela and her latest co-host, Todd Franklin, were discussing the fire, wearing faces that told me they didn't have any personal stake in what happened. Angela had a house, but it wasn't her home. And Todd? He was from the valley. I didn't know if he'd ever even been to Kings Grove.

When the weather came on, Adele turned the volume up a tick.

"Winds have been driving aloft for days, part of what's kept this fire raging forward," Angela said. "But that's all changing today. Take a look at this." The screen flashed to a weather map, showing a massive front moving toward us. "The winds are shifting direction, and bringing with them a certainty of rain," she said. "That's good news for all those who've been fighting this fire for more than a week now."

My heart lifted, and my head snapped to look outside.

"Rain?" Maddie said, standing and following my gaze to the parking lot, which was still a shade of orangey grey.

"Did they say it's going to rain, dear?" Mom was on her feet, at my side with her hair pointing in all directions. I turned to her and tried to tame it with my hands, and then gave her a hug. She hugged me back and whispered in my ear, "Good morning, Little Pudding." It was what she'd said to me every day of my life since I'd been a tiny girl, and hearing the familiar greeting now made something inside me seize up. I hated what I was about to tell her. "Is your dad back?" She let me go and looked around, worry creasing the little lines around her lips.

"No, Mom." I took her hand and led her to the booth where I'd been sleeping. She took a deep breath and slid in next to me.

"What is it?"

"Hal Hammond came in late. I told him not to wake you …"

Mom's eyes widened and her back straightened. She knew what was coming.

"I guess the fire moved last night, advanced with the wind and made some kind of pocket, or something. I didn't really understand, but Dad and Sam …"

My mother's eyes widened and she sucked in a quick breath and took my hand, squeezing it tightly.

"Mom, they're trapped."

She blinked hard and then shook her head. "Trapped?"

"In a hole inside the fire."

"But the hole …"

"Will close up eventually. They're trying to get them out, but we haven't heard anything in a few hours."

Mom looked past me, out the window, where the sliver of orange had faded and the sky had taken on a threatening cast. "Oh God," she murmured.

Chapter 24

SAM

The firefighter, Ryan, and I sat back to back, shielding Mr. George from the advancing flames. The spot where we were trapped was clear enough that there was little to burn, but we could see the walls of fire pulsing, reaching toward one another as the tops of those blazing walls danced ever nearer, trying to connect. It was only a matter of time.

I sat, sweat pouring down my back and my face, my lungs aching as I tried to breathe through the shirt I'd pulled up over my mouth. It was impossible to see beyond the glare of the flames, and after a while I began to lose hope. It felt like all there was in the world was fire. It was all around us, screaming at us, promising a painful, torturous end, and I couldn't imagine a way out. I couldn't see the sky, had no idea what might or might not be happening on the other side of that wall of flame. The firefighter's radio crackled now and then, but it was almost impossible to hear the men on the other side through the noise.

"Sit tight, we're coming," was the last thing I'd heard. They checked in now and then, and the hotshot would confirm we were still alive.

I thought about Miranda most of the time, her sweet face and bright blue eyes. I pictured the way they'd almost always looked at me—a suspicious scowl, usually—and it made me smile. I was so desperate that even her ongoing dislike of me had become a fond memory. I'd give anything to watch her stalk away from me again, even if it meant having to watch her worship my brother for the rest of our lives.

I thought about my brother, too. Chance had picked up a heavy burden when Dad died, coming back though it had never been a part of his plan to return to this tiny mountain town. He came back to shoulder the responsibility of running the business, though I suspected part of the reason he returned was to look after me. Maybe I needed it. Mom had died a long time ago—which didn't mean I didn't miss her. But I'd grown used to that hole in my heart, and our house had become a little colder, a little messier, and a little more practical. No more flowers in vases, no more seasonal decorations. We just lived there together after Chance had gone to school—me and Dad. And it had been okay. But when Dad died...the house had changed again. It was an empty shell I rattled around in. It was good that Chance came back. And now, to think I might not see my big brother again ...

I squeezed my eyes shut tight and waited, trying not to think. I didn't want to get my hopes up that I might get to thank him for coming back, or for stepping back for so many years where Miranda was concerned. I didn't want to think that I might not ever get a chance to take a real shot with the girl I loved. I did my best to shut my brain down and just wait.

"Hey, did you feel that?" Ryan was tapping on my arm, and I opened my eyes.

I looked around, confusion swimming through me. "What? Feel what?" All I could feel was terror and heat.

He didn't say anything else, but stared upward for a long minute. I followed his gaze. The tops of the flames had stopped reaching wildly for each other—in fact the mountains of fire looked smaller, less menacing somehow. And as I gazed upward, a huge fat raindrop landed smack between my eyes.

Rain?

I didn't want to hope. It could just be a passing sprinkle, not enough to help.

But it wasn't. Within minutes, the sky opened and rain was streaming down. It wasn't enough to douse the massive fire, but maybe it would keep it from moving any more for a while. Ryan and I exchanged a hopeful look. Mr. George moved around a bit, and I turned to face him. His eyes hadn't opened, but his chest was still heaving, so I knew he was breathing. We needed to get him out of here before that changed.

Despite the rain, the fire looked as impenetrable as it had before, and though it was a little easier to breathe now that the water was clearing the air a bit, hope was fading as the flames continued to dance around us in defiance of the water. It would have to rain a whole lot harder to put this thing out.

Ryan's radio crackled and we both stared at it as he pulled it from his belt.

"Come in," he shouted. "Come in!"

The radio buzzed to life again, and we heard a string of garbled words, followed by, "Be ready."

We stared at one another, and then scrambled to get to our feet. My legs were weak, and I realized I'd probably inhaled more smoke than was advisable—not that I'd had a choice. I could feel the effects on my body though, and my mind was muddled and slow. I stared at the flames around us, not quite believing what I was seeing as a figure emerged from the fire, stepping into the ever-decreasing circle in which we were trapped. It was another hotshot in full turnout gear, carrying a pile of what looked like clothing in his arms. He dropped it to the ground, and shouted, "Put this on!"

We donned the heavy turnout gear he'd deposited as he explained. "The wind's dying and the rain let us get the fire pretty thin here. We'll have to go through it, and we'd better hurry. The guys are keeping it down on the other side." I stared at him. We were going to walk through the wall of fire?

"And Mr. George?"

The hotshot responded by picking the older man up and throwing him over his shoulder as gently as he could and covering him completely with an open coat. "Let's go!"

Ryan and I exchanged a look and then stepped toward the wall of flame.

"Right there!" The hotshot yelled. "Now!"

I stared at the unyielding wall of dancing fire. Everything in my body was screaming at me to stay put. No one in their right mind walked into fire.

"Go!" He screamed.

I took as deep a breath as I could manage, and forced my legs to move. The heat was incredible, and as I stepped near enough to the flames to touch them, my mind was screaming at me to stop, but I forced my body to keep moving forward into the scorching inferno. I lost all sense of perspective, though I was probably in the fire for only a second or two before emerging on the other side. I couldn't make sense of anything that was happening as the men around me doused me with water, drenching me and then pulling the hot gear from my body. I watched in shock as Ryan and the other hotshot, carrying Mr. George, emerged from a wall of fire and were immediately wet down as I had been.

Consciousness faded in and out, and I heard shouting coming from all sides, but the last thing I remembered was seeing my brother's face above me before everything went black.

Chapter 25
MIRANDA

People began to stir inside the diner not long after I'd told my mom the news, and while our friends and neighbors stretched and yawned, looking around them with wide wondering eyes, Mom stared out the window, unmoving. She'd cried for a little while as we'd sat together in the dissipating darkness, and Maddie had brought her some tea, but whatever processing Mom needed to do to accept the uncertainty all around us, she needed to do it alone. I stayed by her side, my own mind churning in useless circles as I tried to think my father and Sam out of danger.

Adele and Frank appeared at the counter before everyone was awake, and soon muffins, orange juice and hot coffee materialized on the counter and that seemed to bring anyone still sleeping back to consciousness. Worried expressions were exchanged as people sipped coffee, and I slipped into the bathroom at the back of the diner, doing my best to wash my face and smooth my hair back into a ponytail that looked halfway normal.

It felt useless and superficial, worrying about what I looked like when my father and Sam were in so much danger, when everything we loved was threatened. I braced my hands on the sides of the sink and looked at my face in the mirror. Had I aged? Did I look older? Because I felt like I'd been through years in the last few days. I dropped my head between my arms and let the tears come, sucking in the sobs that wanted to roll out of my chest.

I allowed myself a few minutes to fall apart, to imagine a life without my father, to consider moving forward without him. And what terrified me the most was that I could do it. I could picture my mother and me alone in our quiet house—if it still stood. I could see us living quiet lives filled with an unspoken sadness we'd never be able to dispel. And in that image, Sam was gone too, and I knew that the girl I was watching move around in that future inside my head would never be truly happy again.

"No." I sucked in a deep breath and lifted my chin. I wiped at my face and pinched my cheeks. I wasn't giving up. Not on my dad or on Sam. My mother needed me to be strong. Heck, I needed me to be strong. I wasn't a child anymore, and it was time I stepped up and acted like an adult.

But my new resolve crumbled when I stepped out of the bathroom to find my mother sobbing, sitting on the little bench in front of the window outside the bathroom door.

Oh God.

Oh no.

"Mom?" I sank onto the bench next to her, sliding my arm around her shoulders. "Oh God, Mom. Did you hear something? Is—"

My mother turned her head and met my eyes, and I realized she was smiling through her tears. "Look," she said, her voice an amazed whisper. "Look outside, Pudding."

I lifted my head to look out the window behind us, and at

first my mind couldn't process what I saw. The pavement of the small dining plaza was almost black. Was that ash? As my gaze lifted, my mind racing to understand, I realized it was dark with wetness. The chairs and tables outside were dripping and wet, and rain was pouring down from the sky in torrents.

My entire body suddenly felt lighter, the weight of my worry lifting off of me a little bit. And while nothing was assured—we'd had rain two days ago, after all—it was something. Maybe it was a sign, maybe it would buy us time. Maybe it would be enough to allow my father and Sam to escape the fire.

"Have you heard anything?" I asked Mom.

She shook her head, still crying. "But I hope." She didn't add to that. She didn't verbalize what it was she hoped for, and she didn't have to. It was just that. In the dark of the previous night, she hadn't dared to hope, but this morning. She hoped. And so did I.

THAT HOPE WAS a tenuous thread that pulled everyone in the diner through the morning. Conversation was quiet, and we all behaved as if things could be ripped from beneath us at any moment, because realistically, they could.

When Hal Hammond came through the door shortly after eight o'clock, his face was grim, and my heart fell. No good news was delivered when a man looked as somber and morose as Hal.

"Got 'em out," he said without preamble to the diner at large. "Palmer place burned though."

I gasped and my mother did the same at my side, taking my hand and squeezing.

Frank was closest to Hal, and he put an arm on Hal's back and led him to the counter, where Dean slid a cup of coffee in front of him. Hal shook his head and his shoulders hunched for a minute as he sat, and then he seemed to recover himself. "So far that's the only local structure."

My mother stepped near to Hal and sank onto the stool next to him, everything in her body language careful and hesitant. "Hal?" she whispered.

The older man turned to look at her, and his face showed all the worry, the work, the exhaustion he felt. But his eyes widened and he nodded at her. "They're out," he said. "They got them out." He swung his gaze to me. "They're meeting the ambulance here. Gonna take 'em down to Kings General."

Mom's eyes widened and she glanced at the parking lot out the windows. "Now? Where are they? Are they okay?" Her voice was thin and rising.

Hal probably could have planned his news-sharing more thoughtfully, but I could see how tired and overwhelmed he was. He put a hand on my mother's arm, and she quieted down. "I think so, Mrs. George, but I don't know for sure." He turned to the windows and stood. "Coming in now."

Flashing lights strobed the windows of the diner as an ambulance pulled up out front. A fire truck pulled in just behind it, turning into the lot from the opposite direction. I held my breath as Mom and I rushed out into the rain.

We stood holding hands on the sidewalk as the rain poured around us, soaking our clothes immediately and sticking our hair to our scalps. The strange thing was that I didn't feel any of it as I watched the men pull Dad and Sam from the truck. Dad was on a stretcher, and his eyes were closed. As soon as I saw him, my heart leapt into my throat and my knees threatened to go. He wasn't moving.

The paramedics rushed to him and Mom stood back, a hand to her mouth and her eyes wide as she watched them transfer him to the back of the ambulance. I pulled her to the doors. "This is his wife," I told them, and they reached down to pull her into the back of the ambulance.

"He's stable," the paramedic said, and I watched my mother take my father's hand and lean down over his body, her back shaking.

Relief poured through me. He was alive. My dad was alive, though his hands were wrapped in bandages, and his face was blackened beneath the oxygen mask. The doors to the ambulance were closed, and it turned around slowly in the parking lot and then pulled out, my parents disappearing down the road in the rain.

A big hand fell on my shoulder and I turned to find Chance Palmer standing next to me. "He's going to be all right," he said. "He took in a lot of smoke, but I'm sure he'll be all right."

I looked up at him gratefully. "Where's Sam?" I asked, looking around. My eyes had been fixed to my father's prone form, but now they found Sam, sitting on the curb at the edge of the parking lot, holding a bottle of water and shaking his head at a paramedic.

"He's busy arguing with the guys trying to help him. He's fine," he said, and he stepped back.

I stared at Sam, my heart twisting inside my chest and my skin warming as I realized how happy I was to see him, how relieved I was to find him safe. But more than that, I felt a surge of warmth inside me when those stormy eyes met mine, when he stood and walked toward me, ignoring whatever the paramedic was saying to him.

My feet moved without me being conscious of having decided to go to him, and seconds later, I was swept up into his strong arms, my body pressed thankfully against his broad solid chest. I clasped my arms around his neck, and he swung me around again, just as he'd done the day it had rained after we'd wrapped cabins together. Only this time, when he leaned down to kiss me, I wasn't confused. I pressed myself up to him, relishing every centimeter of contact we shared, knowing that when his lips met mine, it was exactly what I wanted and everything I needed.

The rain was coming down in torrents, and our bodies were slick with it, water streaming from our noses and fingertips as we ended the kiss and stood holding one another, looking into the depths of one another's eyes. There were so many things I wanted to say to Sam, so many things I wanted to ask him about the past, but maybe none of it mattered. In that moment, it certainly didn't. All that mattered right then was that he was safe. He and my father were safe, and the way the rain was sheeting down, I wondered if maybe the village was safe too.

"I'm so happy to see you," I whispered in his ear, almost missing the gentle waft of licorice that usually clung to him. Now he smelled like smoke and the verdant mossy wetness surrounding us both.

He responded by finding my lips again, and I closed my eyes and let myself be comforted by the kiss and the arms of the man I realized I'd probably loved in some way my whole life.

"Sir, you're going to need to get in the ambulance," the paramedic said from somewhere far, far away.

Sam and I broke apart to find the man standing just inches from us, and as I took a step back from Sam, the rest of the scene around us came back into focus.

"Yes," I said. "Go with him, Sam. Let's make sure you're all right."

He shook his head. "I'm fine. And we have things to talk about."

"We have time," I said. "Go now, they're waiting for you."

"Go to the hospital, moron," Chance said, stepping close to persuade his brother.

"If you come," Sam said, turning to me.

I nodded and gave Chance a smile, and we got into the ambulance—Sam in the back and me up front—and headed down to the hospital. As we pulled out of the lot, I looked out the window to see Chance standing alone in the rain, his hands stuffed into his pockets as he watched us go.

Chapter 26

SAM

Going to the hospital when there's nothing wrong with you has to rank up there pretty high on the list of stupid pointless things that get in the way of what you'd really like to be doing. For me, the priority was getting a chance to talk to Miranda, but it turned out that when your home has just burned to the ground, your community has just narrowly dodged a fiery bullet, and you're being treated for smoke inhalation, it's nearly impossible to find a quiet moment to pour your heart out to the woman you've loved your whole life ... who you might actually have a chance with.

Miranda had come to the hospital with me, which should have been a surprise. In the world we'd lived in before the fire, that wouldn't ever have happened. Not in a million years.

But in the world since the fire? Something had shifted. The misunderstandings and aggravations of our youth had been burned away. Or maybe we'd just realized there wasn't time for the bullshit. There was way too much at stake.

We didn't get a chance to talk, to really talk, because Miranda was darting between my ER cubicle and the room to which her father had been admitted, and none of us had really slept in days. So even if words were something we'd needed during that time, they probably would've been hard to come by. But the things between us that were unspoken carried us forward, and when I stared into those bright blue eyes while the doctor checked my vitals and asked me questions, I knew that my world had changed in more ways than I could number.

And it was funny that despite losing so much in the fire, I felt as if it had really given me more than I'd ever really dared to hope for.

Chapter 27
MIRANDA

Dad was going to be okay. And that meant that Mom was going to be okay, and so was I. They kept him for two days and performed a procedure to clear his airways of debris and detect further damage, but declared him good to leave once he'd awoken and spent one more night to demonstrate his breathing function was restored. We came right back up the hill, even though the doctors suggested a few days at a lower altitude would be good for him.

At home, Mom treated him like a king, plumping pillows behind him and bringing his favorite tuna sandwiches and Coke on a little platter he could balance on his lap while he watched television. Despite the amount of work the Park Service had to do to clean up in the aftermath of the fire's near miss with the village, Dad had been given a short leave of absence to recuperate.

Though the fire still wasn't one hundred percent contained, the leading edge—the one that threatened us—had been contained, and the firefighters were close to putting out the bulk of what still burned in the backcountry. The weather remained blessedly cool and agreeable in the wake of the storm that had turned the tide, and while we didn't get a lot more rain after the twenty-four hour storm, it had made all the difference in giving us the upper hand.

Sam's health had been cleared the first day, while I'd stayed with my dad in the hospital. Sam had returned to Kings Grove to be with Chance and handle details of the business, and their lost home. We'd shared a quick kiss goodbye, and the way Sam's hand lingered on mine as he'd turned to go told me there were conversations in our future, things that needed to be said.

I texted Sam on my way back up the hill, letting him know we were coming back, and he asked if I'd be able to meet him that night.

ME: Definitely (this was typed as a mad flurry of nerves jumped around inside me). *Where?*
Sam: I'd say my place, but...
Me: I'm so sorry, Sam.
Sam: Office?
Me: Sure. When?
Sam: Seven?
Me: Deal.

I ATE dinner with my family, the mood between us strangely sweet and gentle after all that'd we had faced and almost lost. Despite the quiet goodness floating around us at home, I couldn't seem to keep still.

We'd begun reheating some of the food Mom had maniacally put in the freezer, and were at the table when Dad shot me a meaningful look.

"Pudding."

I snapped out of a daze I hadn't even realized I was in. "Sorry, what?"

"You're causing an earthquake."

My leg had been bouncing up and down, nerves jittering through my body as I anticipated going to the Palmer offices to meet Sam. "Sorry, Dad." I stilled my bouncing leg and Dad took his hand off his water glass, which had been dancing across the table as I'd jostled it.

"What's up?" He asked. His voice was still hoarse from the smoke he'd inhaled, but he had begun to look more rested and relaxed.

"I'm going to go talk to Sam in a few minutes."

"That poor boy," Mom said. "I just feel awful for those two," she continued, seeming to miss the point of my meeting and my nerves. "They've lost so much. First their mother and then their dad, and then Chance told me about the horrible thing that had happened with his fiancée down there in Fresno …" She shook her head and wiped her eyes. Mom had been on the brink of tears every moment since the fire.

"What did you just say?" My mind finally skipped past the event on my own horizon. "About Chance? A fiancée?"

She nodded solemnly. "He told me about it just a week or so ago. His grad school girlfriend. They were going to be married."

"I don't think even Sam knows about that," I said, doubting that Sam would have suggested I had a shot with his brother if he'd had any idea he'd just lost someone. My heart, already so raw and exposed, ached for Chance.

"What happened, Mom?"

"A car accident, I think. Just after his father died."

"Oh my God," I whispered.

The tears had begun to streak my mother's soft face again, so I let the topic slide away, not wanting to see her cry any more. When the clock finally ticked toward seven, I rose. "I have to go."

"Drive safe, honey," Dad said, and he stood to kiss my cheek and walk me to the door. "Love you."

It was a strange positive outcome of a horrific event, but the fire had led us all to spend more time ensuring we told those around us what they meant to us. Even Adele had been friendly when I'd dropped by the diner the day before.

I drove my little truck through the village, my heart slowly accelerating as I neared the Palmer office. Sam's red truck was parked out front, and I could see the light glowing through the high window in his office.

I STEPPED through the door of the office, feeling more nervous than I had since I'd had to climb onto that stage at the prom. I could hardly believe the same butterflies that had been so mindlessly devoted to Chance Palmer for so many years were willing to shift their loyalty so easily to his brother Sam. I guess I could understand where they were coming from. I'd done the same thing.

The office was lit in a warm glow by the single lamp on my desk, and the light shining into the lobby from Sam's open door.

"Hello?" I called, closing the front door behind me.

Sam appeared in his office doorway, almost stumbling as he crossed the threshold. He looked nervous, crossing his arms and grinning at me with a lock of hair falling into his eyes. "Hi," he said, then cleared his throat. "It's good, um, I mean …" He uncrossed his arms and shoved a hand through the hair in his face. "I'm glad you're here." He stopped moving and just stood looking at me.

I felt my face flame red and was suddenly aware of my own

hands, which had nowhere to go. I tried to shove my car keys into my bag, and naturally, missed. They fell to the floor in a jangling heap, and I was almost relieved to have a task to focus on, even if picking up my keys would only take a second.

I stood back up and faced Sam. "You're doing okay?" I asked.

"Yeah," he said. "Come in." He stepped back into his office, and waved toward the couch against the wall.

When we were both sitting, facing each other, silence settled around us, heavy with expectation.

"I'm so sorry about your house," I said, unable to look him in the face for some reason. I stared at my hands, which acknowledged my heartfelt gaze by twitching in my lap.

"Yeah," Sam said, and it was almost a sigh. "I mean, it's okay. It's not, but ... we've got rooms at the Inn."

"Oh," I managed.

What the hell was wrong with me?

"Why is this so weird?" I asked, figuring the uncomfortable air between us might dissipate if we acknowledged it. "I'm all discombobulated and anxious." I tucked a leg beneath me, still unable to meet Sam's eye.

"I know," he said, his voice low. "I am too." The timbre of his voice was sandy and smoky, and though it was also familiar, the feelings it brought to life inside me were not. I was giddy and jumpy, hot and nervous. I didn't know what to do with my fingers, my eyes. I could barely breathe.

How the hell were we ever going to be able to talk if I couldn't even figure out how to breathe? Doubt began to creep in. This was Sam, for God's sake. Maybe we were both nuts to believe anything could actually work between us. We'd had too many years of being at odds.

I stared at my fingers in my lap, twisting around each other.

"This might help." That voice stirred me up again, but I didn't lift my eyes. That's why it took me completely off guard when suddenly Sam was there, on his knees in front of me. He reached out a hand and cupped my jaw, and I dared a glance at him. His eyes were dark, his mouth slightly open. His gaze fell to my mouth and he leaned in. Sam didn't hesitate, he ignored the awkward tension between us, and I heard him inhale sharply just before his lips touched mine, and in that instant, everything else disappeared.

I felt Sam's other hand wrap around the back of my neck, pulling me farther into him, into the kiss. The heat created by our lips pressing softly together melted into me, slowly trickling through my torso, my limbs. And as I opened my lips to Sam's teasing tongue, the frazzled tension inside me dissipated, replaced immediately by a different kind of tension. I pressed my body into Sam, slipping to the floor so that we were both on our knees, our bodies molding together, hands pulling the other nearer. In that kiss, I said so many things I'd been too nervous to admit to Sam, I told him how much I'd been wrong about, how blind I'd been for so long.

After a few long blissful minutes, his hands still cupping my face, Sam pulled away. His chest rose and fell, and his eyes stayed on mine, dark and deep. But the slow silly grin that spread gradually across his face was familiar in contrast to this new sexy version of the boy I'd grown up alongside. It was Sam, and while the parts of me that had been nervous coming in here threatened to spring back to the surface, now that familiarity was mixed with something else—a deep attraction and a desire to get to know what lay behind the familiar exterior.

"Sam, I—" I started, but Sam's mouth collided with mine again. This time the kiss was urgent and hot, but it was over quickly, and then Sam was pulling me to my feet, laughing.

"Okay," he said, his grin anchoring me to him. "Now we can talk."

I couldn't help but laugh, my hand still folded in his as we sat.

"I owe you an apology," I said, holding his gaze and feeling the confidence of our mutual desire pushing me to be truthful. "For so much."

The grin dropped in wattage, but one side of his mouth stayed curled up in a sexy smile and he laughed. "You don't," he said.

"I was so oblivious. For so long." I hated thinking about all the time I'd wasted, staring after Chance. I'd been like a silly girl in a jewelry store, unable to see the value of a gorgeous handcrafted piece because I was too busy being blinded by the diamonds. "It's just, we've known each other so long, Sam, and I thought I knew exactly what I wanted."

"Hey," Sam interrupted me. "What do you want now?"

I held his gaze, my heart swelling as I stared at the boy who'd been there my entire life, and I realized that was exactly why he was where I was meant to be. Sam had always been there. He'd stood by as I fumbled through my life, picking me up when I fell down (even if he chuckled as he did it), and setting me back on my path. He'd stood by and waited patiently, steadfast and loyal.

"I think I want you." I heard the amazement in my voice, and saw the light dim slightly in Sam's eyes.

"You think, huh?" His grip on my hand lessened and he sat up straighter, putting space between us.

"But you told me you were going to leave Kings Grove. And now that your house is gone ..." my voice faded as I thought about the reality of Sam leaving town.

"Things change," he said. "Anything can change." He dropped my hand and my gaze, and a chill washed through me.

I wanted to fill the space between us again, replace the chill with something, eradicate the void. But Sam cleared his throat and then spoke again.

"Miranda, I've known you my whole life. And I've had a crush on you almost as long."

My heart swelled, but I was afraid to hope. If Sam left, I wasn't sure what would be left here for me.

"And I've waited for you to figure it out, to decide that maybe the nice guy was the guy you wanted." He took a breath, meeting my eyes again. "But I'm tired of waiting, Miranda. I know there's something between us, and I know it could be more. People don't develop the kind of aggravation we share, they don't drive each other batty like we do, if there's nothing there."

His words lingered in my mind and I turned them over, examining them for truth.

"Miranda," he said, pulling my eyes back to his and putting a soft hand beneath my chin. "I love you. I always have. And I don't want to wait for you anymore. I don't want to stand by and be the nice guy hoping to win the girl. I'm sitting here now, asking you, right now—do you want to be with me? Do you see a future for us? Because if you do, that changes everything.

"If you think we might share a future together, might have something worth keeping, then I have no reason to leave Kings Grove."

"But your house ..." I had no idea why I was looking for reasons for him to go. My heart was rebelling inside my chest, absorbing his words, testing them for truth. And finding them valid.

"I know some guys in construction," he said, his lips curling into that sexy half smile again. "The house isn't an issue. Besides, maybe it's time Chance and I each have our own house."

Still unable to form actual intelligent words, I began nodding, my hands reaching for Sam again.

"Miranda," he said. "I need to hear you say it. Tell me it's worth the risk. Is there something here? Am I crazy to think there is?"

I went from wild nodding to erratic head shaking, and finally found my tongue again. "No. No, definitely no."

"No?" Sam pulled his hand from mine, dropped his palm from my chin.

"No, you're not crazy," I clarified, taking his hand back. "You're not crazy. This thing between us—" I motioned between us, "—this is probably crazy. But maybe that's why it makes so much sense. And it took me so long to realize it, and I'm so sorry."

"Stop apologizing to me."

"But I am … you've been there for me. My whole life, you've been here, and I was too blind to realize it. I mean, even in high school. And," I felt myself flush again, and cringed as I realized what was about to come out of my mouth. But he'd been a part of the most humiliating moment I could remember, and I needed to know how to think about that in the context of this new reality between us. "I mean, you were there in the shed … and on that stage …" I broke eye contact and shook my head. The shame I felt was so familiar, and I'd felt it for so long I couldn't shake it off.

"Miranda, it's okay." His voice was soft, and he squeezed my hand.

"When everyone else was laughing at me, you were there, you were trying to help up on that stage. And you never told me about the shed because …"

"Because I would have had to tell you why I was there."

"But you were there … for me." It wasn't a question really, but I needed to put all the events I thought had defined me into context. To understand Sam's real role in them.

I raised my gaze to his, and the warmth I saw in his eyes gave me comfort.

"I was there because I was in love with you." Sam sighed. "My feelings for you aren't new, Miranda. I've loved you since high school. Maybe longer. Maybe I fell in love with you that day when I watched the way you scrambled around on the floor in first grade trying to rescue those goldfish."

I scooted closer to Sam on the couch, looking at our hands connected on my lap and letting his words warm me. "I don't care about high school, about the past. I just don't want you to leave now. I want to see what this is between us, to have a chance together."

"You do?" Sam's voice was husky and low.

"I was distracted, Sam. I was stupid and confused, and I'm so sorry. But when you were back there in the fire, when I thought you might not come back, I realized I needed to tell you. Even with the licorice—"

"The licorice?"

"The awful licorice," I said. "Even with the licorice, I still love you. I think maybe I always have."

The grin broke out again, and my heart leapt. I pressed myself into his arms and wrapped my arms around his neck. "Just tell me you're going to stay," I said.

"I'll stay," he said, smiling down at me. "I'll stay forever if I get to be with you."

Sam pressed his lips to mine again, and we fell backwards onto the couch, and I felt everything I never knew I wanted click into place inside me. The air in the room seemed to heat and condense until Sam and I were wrapped in a delicious little bubble that was only us and everything in the world all at once. Happiness swelled in my cells even as my muscles tensed and my stomach flipped at the way Sam's mouth claimed mine.

He hovered above me on the couch, supported on his elbow as I lay on my back. His mouth was like magic, his tongue and lips coaxing sensations from my skin I didn't even know were possible. I'd had sex—a couple less-than-thrilling experiences with a boy who'd come up to work in the intern ranger program one summer after high school—but it wasn't anything I thought much about. But even just kissing Sam had my head spinning. And when his mouth traced soft teasing lines down my jaw and over my throat, my whole body tingled as my mind threatened to unleash from its moorings.

His hand traced my hip and found the skin of my stomach as he kissed me, and I couldn't help the gasp that flew out of me when that hand traced a path up to my breast. I clutched his hard firm back harder as his thumb grazed my nipple, his mouth working at the base of my throat. His knee had slid between mine, and I pushed myself up against him, his firm thigh pressing into my center as I arched. Sam's erection was hard against my hip as I writhed beneath him, and my mind reeled, trying to keep track of everything I was feeling, how shocking it was that Sam could make me feel this way.

I grew bolder, my hands reaching and pulling, grabbing at his ass, pulling his shirt off over his head. Sam pulled back from kissing me to stare at me for a long moment after his shirt was in a pile on the floor and a sexy smile spread slowly over his face. My hands explored the firm smooth planes of his bare chest. "I wish I could memorize every second of this," he said, his voice a rough whisper. "It's so much better than my fantasies."

"How about if we just do it often enough that you won't need to remember?" I suggested, struggling to remove my own shirt as I lay trapped in Sam's arms.

He grinned and pulled me up to sit, then slowly unfastened each button down my chest, his big fingers working carefully as his eyes danced. When he'd pulled the shirt from my body, he took a deep long breath, as if he needed to steady himself as he looked at me sitting there in my black bra.

"God, you're pretty," he said, shaking his head a little bit as his big hands cupped my shoulders delicately.

I'd lost the ability to speak, my mouth suddenly dry at the sight of Sam's broad smooth chest, his muscled stomach, the bulging girth of his biceps. I dropped my hands to his belt and slowly pulled it from his pants as his eyes tracked every motion of my hands.

Without agreeing to do so, we both stood, and helped each other out of the remainder of our clothes. And then, after a brief pause, Sam's hands wrapped my back, slipped down to my ass to lift me to settle on his hips, and walked me back against the door of his office. He uttered one word, low and reverent before he kissed me senseless again: "fuuuck."

With only a quick break to pull a condom from his wallet, Sam did exactly that, right there against the door. I had thought to complain for a quick second when he left me standing there cold, but there was something about being lifted off the floor in those incredible arms, about being held in place by his sheer desire.

By the time he lined himself up, seeking my consent with wide beautiful blue-gray eyes and a question on lips red and swollen from kissing me, I wanted him to fuck me against that door more than I'd wanted anything in the world. And when he pressed inside me, slowly and carefully, I was squirming and thrashing in his arms to get more.

"Yes," I heard myself moaning while Sam thrust deeply into me, his hands on my ass and my back against the hard unyielding wood. "Oh god, yes." I was nearly senseless, so full and surrounded by Sam and the scent of sex and black licorice and the mountains, I couldn't think of anything but that moment, of the way he held me and the sound of his breath, and the feel of his thick hard cock driving me higher.

"Miranda," he breathed, his head against my neck, his breath hot against my skin. "God, Miranda, you're so …" He didn't say anything else, his body making it clear exactly what he was thinking, feeling. And his desire and excitement spiked my own until I felt everything inside me coiling, tightening, squeezing in preparation for a release I worried might actually shatter me.

"Oh god, Sam, I'm gonna—" I didn't get the words out before my body unleashed, spiraling outward in delicious waves centered only by his hands holding me to the earth and his cock pinning me to the door. Through the pulsating sensations, I heard him groan and felt the urgency of his thrusts increase until his hands gripped me tighter and I felt him pulse inside me.

After what could have been seconds or minutes or maybe a decade, I began to come back to myself, and I marveled at the fact that I was in Sam's arms, here in the Palmer office, enjoying the afterglow of the best sex I'd ever had.

Sam's arms wrapped me tightly, and he walked us both over to the couch and set me down, lying by my side. His hands traced the lines of my body as his eyes tracked my face, the sexy smile holding fast on his lips.

"Aren't you going to say anything?" I asked him. Sam was always ready with a quip.

"I'm speechless, I guess," he said. "I just got everything I've ever wanted, and you're still here, in my arms. It's more than I ever dreamed about. I'm just trying to figure out if it's real."

Joy fluttered through me on paperthin wings. "It's real," I promised him. And then I kissed him hard and pulled all the hard firm ridges and planes of Sam Palmer against me again. It turned out it was everything I'd ever wanted too, I just hadn't known it before.

We rested and then Sam was kissing me again, and for the next few hours, we were a tangle of limbs and lips, and hands and heat. And there was nowhere else I wanted to be.

Chapter 28
MIRANDA

The house was dark when I arrived home that night, and I tiptoed through the door, feeling a sense of mystified rightness. It was crazy to me in so many ways that just days ago, my entire world was falling apart and everything felt so wrong. And now, especially tonight, everything felt completely solid and cohesive. If someone had told me years ago—or even days ago—that Sam Palmer and I would fall in love, that we'd maybe always been in love, I would have told them they were nuts. But now? I'd never felt like anything had ever made more sense. The smile smeared across my face felt good, and my heart felt light.

"There you are," my mother said, her voice echoing out of the mostly dark room. I jumped and my hand flew to my heart. I hadn't seen her sitting there in the corner, bent over her planner with her multicolored pens spread around her on the table.

"You scared the crap out of me, Mom!" I walked to where she sat, looking around in confusion. Something had changed, but I wasn't sure exactly what it was. "What are you doing up?"

She was giving me a very smug look, and I had the feeling

she knew exactly what had kept me out so late. "Should I ask you the same question?"

"I'd rather if you didn't."

"How's Sam Palmer?"

I couldn't help the grin that popped back onto my face. I wanted to tell her that I loved him, that I was the happiest girl in the world, that it felt like the universe had shifted overnight and now I could see it in ways I'd never seen it before. But I wasn't about to tell my mother all the things I'd just done with Sam on the couch in his office. "He's good," I said instead.

Mom smiled up at me, and I could see that I didn't need to explain anything. She already knew.

My mother stood up and closed her planner, scooping up the pens and depositing them on top of the book. That was when I realized what was different. The puzzle was completed beneath her work on the table. Staring out from the center of the finished tableau was a picture of our house, with my family standing in front of it. The picture had been taken when I was only four, and my hair was wild and curly and sticking up in every direction. My mom had the puzzle made soon after the picture was taken, and it had been on this table for the last few years at least—since one of us had gotten the idea to do it and then abandoned it somewhere along the way. It was amazing no pieces were missing. "You finished the puzzle," I said.

"We did. Your dad and I did it before he turned in tonight."

I studied our faces as they looked back up at us from the tabletop. We looked happy. We looked young. "I love this picture," I said,

Mom wrapped an arm around my shoulders and tilted her head to touch mine. "Me too."

"What have you been doing, Mom? Planning?"

She turned her head and grinned at me. "Angela Snow called this evening," she said. "She wants me to take a weekly spot on their new morning show. They're extending for an hour after Good Morning Kings Grove to do a lifestyle show, and they want someone to give household tips on everything from organization to goal setting." Mom blushed and then added. "She called me. Even after SheetGate."

"Mom! That's amazing." I hadn't thought I could possibly feel happier, but my chest swelled and joy made me throw my arms around my mother and squeeze her tightly. "You'll be perfect for that."

A moment of doubt crossed her features as she pulled back to look at me. "Well," she said. "No one is really perfect, but I'm going to do the best I can."

"You'll do great, Mom."

We stood together looking at the puzzle for a minute longer, and then Mom squeezed my hand and said goodnight.

I went upstairs feeling like everything in my life had grown and evolved, and I couldn't wait to go to work the next morning.

Chapter 29

SAM

It didn't take long for Chance and I to get going to work in the morning—one benefit of living across the parking lot from the office. We'd stopped in at the diner for breakfast on our way over, and while I was in the habit of looking around for Miranda's car in the lot every time I went to the diner, I already knew she wasn't going to be in this morning. I smiled as I thought about the situation I'd been in when I'd thought to ask about schedules for the next day. Miranda had been beneath me on the couch, her shirt in a pile on the floor and her blond hair spilling all around us as I'd kissed her over and over again. I couldn't believe she was mine to kiss, mine to touch. *Mine.*

"Better quit it or your face will freeze that way," Chance said as we settled into a booth and thanked Maddie for the coffee. It seemed like every ounce of happiness I'd found since the night the fire turned had been suctioned directly from my brother's soul. He frowned into his mug and I wished—not for the first time—that we were the kind of brothers who really talked.

"Can't help it. I'm happy."

He squinted up at me and then ducked his chin again, muttering, "You deserve it, bro. Waited long enough."

I leaned back in the booth and let myself enjoy the way my excitement seemed to heighten every sound around us, amplify every color and sensation. "Thanks," I said, wishing he seemed happier.

We ordered our breakfasts, which was really just an exercise since we rarely ordered anything different and Maddie could probably just bring us the usual and keep things simple. And then I decided to try to talk to my brother. He was clearly hurting, and though we'd never really had heartfelt chats, there was a first time for everything.

"You okay, Chance?"

He blew out a harsh breath that was halfway between a laugh and a grunt. "Yeah. Fine."

I crossed my arms. "We could talk about it."

He pressed his lips together and looked up at me, assessing. "Yeah? I don't think I have a story you'll want to hear. Especially not while you're enjoying that post-coital glow you've got going on."

"I didn't say we—" I stopped. It wasn't Chance's business what Miranda and I had or hadn't done. "Talk to me, Chance."

He shook his head, and laughed bitterly. Then his voice dropped low and pain rolled out with his words, thick and raw. "Just feels like a lot of losing lately, you know? Like maybe I'll never get another win."

I tried not to look incredulous. "Chance. Seriously? I think if there's an illustrated dictionary around here anywhere I can prove you wrong. Next to the word 'winner' is a picture of you."

"Yeah." The word dismissed the conversation, and Chance chuckled bitterly. "Right."

I needed to let him talk. I tried again. "Tell me."

"You were there, Sam. Mom died."

"That was a long time ago." Chance had been sixteen when Mom died, in his sophomore year at high school.

"Yeah. It was. But Mom died, and then Dad …"

"Yeah," I agreed. "It sucks." It did. Not having our parents to witness our adult lives felt unfair and cruel, but I didn't spend a lot of time thinking about it now and it surprised me to hear Chance did.

"But there's been more than that," he said. "I haven't told you."

I waited, worry pulling itself into a twisty ball inside my chest. What didn't I know? What could be so bad it would make my all-American brother crumble like this? "What?"

"Rebecca." He said the name quietly, reverently. "A month before Dad." It was a whisper.

"Rebecca?"

"My fiancée."

Shock made me sit up straight. "What?" We might not have shared quiet chats often, but I thought we did share the big stuff, things like the, 'hey there, little brother, I'm getting married' kind of stuff. "Fiancée?"

"I didn't even get time to tell you. She was in a car accident."

"What?" It turned out that shock made me a shitty conversationalist.

"And now the house." He rubbed the back of his neck and leaned heavily on his elbows over the table, looking as close to beaten as I'd ever seen him. "It's just … it's a lot."

I reached out and put a hand on my brother's shoulder, which made him jump at first and then he lifted his head and met my eye. We sat like that for a while, just sharing the quiet moment, saying the things we hadn't been able to actually speak.

"Sorry," he said, shaking off my hand as the food arrived.

"Chance," I said, waiting until he looked up at me again. "I'm sorry. And if you ever want to talk about it …"

"I don't."

We ate in relative silence, and as our plates were cleared, Chance's back seemed a little straighter, his face a little clearer. "What do you want to do about the house?"

"I want to rebuild," I said. "I'm not going anywhere."

He nodded. "Me either."

Surprise washed through me. "You're staying? What about going down to Fresno? Starting something bigger in the valley?"

"Just told you, Sam. I'm tired of losing things. I'm staying here with you. And when you and George pop out little Palmer-Georges, I'm going to be right there, spoiling the shit out of them and being their all-time favorite uncle."

I didn't know I'd been worried about Chance leaving, but hearing that he planned to stay made me happier than I'd expected it would. I grinned. "Maybe we should build two houses?"

"You don't want to live with your big brother forever and ever?"

"It's tempting, but I'm done washing your smelly socks and picking up your dishes."

"You love taking care of me," he joked. "Yeah … two houses. Think we can get it through approvals?"

I thought about that. You could rebuild a structure that had been destroyed, but expanding it by much sometimes met with resistance from the approval board. "Well, we did have that old shed down the hill."

Chance nodded slowly. "Yeah …"

"So we rebuild the house. And the shed."

"Which one of us gets to live in a tool shed?" he asked, a smile pulling one side of his face up as his eyes gleamed.

"You?" I tried.

"You're the tool."

And we'd arrived back at our usual level of maturity.

"If we did it right, the shed could be a pretty cool little two-story setup," he said.

"If only we knew a talented architect."

Chance threw a pancake at me and stood, looking a little bit brighter and happier than he had this morning. I accepted the syrup stain on my pants as fair trade for my brother's lighter mood. "Go draw us some houses," he said. "I've gotta take care of some things down in the valley."

The way he said it made me think it had something to do with the mysterious fiancée I'd never heard of before, and I wondered if maybe Chance was still seeking some kind of closure there. I wished I'd had a chance to meet the woman who'd managed to get Chance to propose, but I wasn't going to push right now. "Okay," I said, and I finished my breakfast and then headed out of the diner under a bright blue sky without even a hint of smoke in the air.

"Sam!" A thin voice wafted toward me as I walked the narrow path that led from the lot to Palmer.

I turned to see Mrs. Teague's small frame next to her old white Volvo.

I didn't see Mrs. Teague much around town, but today she looked thin and small standing by her car. I turned and trotted back to her side. "How are you, Mrs. Teague? Did you go down the hill to evacuate?"

She shook her head and looked sad. "No, Sam. I figured if the house was going, I was going too."

Shock sifted through me. What a morbid thought. It occurred to me suddenly that Mrs. Teague wasn't just a little old lady who liked to get a bit handsy with the help. She was lonely—maybe terminally so. "Oh, Mrs. Teague," I managed, unsure what to say. "Well, is the house okay? Anything need fixing? I could come around this afternoon."

She smiled up at me. "You're such a good boy, Sam. And that's exactly what I came to talk to you about. I'm going to refurbish the second floor," she said. "My grandchildren are going to be coming up for Christmas, and then they're going to spend summers up here with me."

"That's great," I said, the thought of kids keeping her busy making me happy.

"So I need you to come by and see what needs doing."

"I can definitely do that, Mrs. Teague," I told her. "This afternoon then?"

"Whenever is convenient, Sam. I know you're busy."

I leaned down and kissed her on the cheek. "I'll be by around three," I promised.

She glowed and smiled at me as I walked away, heading for the office where I knew Miranda was waiting for me.

I COULDN'T REMEMBER EVER HAVING BEEN nervous walking through the door of Palmer in the morning for work, but I imagined now that Miranda George and I were ... whatever we were ... lots of things would be different. I took a deep breath and walked into the lobby, to find her sitting behind her desk, blond hair piled on top of her head, and her dark-framed glasses perched down at the end of her nose as she stared at her screen.

When she heard me come in, her eyes widened and a bright smile lit up her beautiful face. "Sam." The way she said my name made my heart leap. There was a soft reverence in her voice I'd never heard before, and to know that it was directed at me had parts of my body springing to attention with glee.

"Hey," I said, unable to manage much more because my

heart was trying to expand to ninety times its normal size inside my chest.

She stood and came around her desk, looking slightly uncertain for the briefest second as she pressed herself into my arms. I wrapped her in an embrace and her hands on my back felt like validation, like heaven, like everything I'd ever wanted. I was hit with a wave of gratitude so strong it nearly leveled me. I'd waited my whole life for this, for this girl to finally look up and see me waiting here. And today? I was holding her in my arms.

"I'm so happy to see you," she said, her head nestled against my chest.

I tightened my grip on her. "This is my favorite day ever so far," I told her.

That made her laugh and tilt her head back to look up at me, the bright blue eyes dancing. "Why? Did something happen already?"

"You're here," I said, feeling totally unable to explain how completely overwhelmed I was by everything.

She kissed my chin, since she wasn't quite tall enough to reach my cheek, and I leaned down and pressed my lips to hers. For a little while, we just stood in the front lobby of the office and kissed, and eventually she loosened her grip and smiled at me again. "I think we have actual work to do."

I nodded. "I have to design myself a new house," I said. "And one for Chance."

Her eyebrows shot up. "You're both staying?"

"This is our home," I said, thinking of Chance's face this morning. "We belong here, both of us."

She nodded.

"But maybe not in the same house."

"It'll be so weird for you—you've always been together."

"We'll be on the same lot, but we need a little distance." I thought about Chance's misery this morning. "I don't mind having him next door, though. I'm hoping maybe you'll help me build something you might like to live in one day," I told her, still a little bit afraid to put too much of my heart out.

She sucked in a quick breath and then grinned wildly. "Can I help?"

"Yeah," I said, taking her hand. "Come see the ideas I have." I'd been designing my dream house for years.

"Did I tell you I only have one more credit and I'll have my design degree?" She said it quietly, and I stopped walking and stared at her.

"No. I had no idea you'd done so much. That's great." An idea began to form in my mind, but I didn't want to overwhelm the girl. I'd told her I loved her and asked her to design a house to share with me all in the space of twenty-four hours. Maybe asking her to be a partner in the business would be too much in the same day. I swallowed down the question and managed a half-crazy grin instead. "Then you'll design all the interiors and consult as we build."

It was Miranda's turn to grin.

I set my bag down at my desk as she walked to my drafting table and began turning pages. I heard her lift one page after another, and then realized what I'd left on the bottom sheet with a flush of embarrassment. "Oh, hey, hold on—"

But it was too late. Miranda stood, staring at her own face looking back up at her. I'd been drawing Miranda for years. She was actually the first thing I'd ever really tried to draw. I felt blood rush into my cheeks and I stepped slowly to her side, wondering what she would think.

"You've been drawing me," she said, but she didn't sound surprised.

"You're beautiful," I said. It was all the explanation I could manage.

She stared down at the sheet, which showed her profile, focused on a close study of her eyes, and had a full body drawing of her laughing down at the bottom. "These are amazing. We should frame them."

"You don't mind?"

Her gaze lifted to meet mine, and she laughed, a breathy noise that pulled at the muscles low in my stomach. "I love that you see me this way, that you see me as ... beautiful."

"I don't think there's any other way to see you," I told her, and I wrapped an arm around her and kissed her cheek before bending down to get the plans I'd been working on for years—my dream home.

I rolled out the plans, and Miranda made appreciative noises, moving her finger gingerly through the rooms, picking up details here and there.

"I love this," she said.

We spent most of the rest of that day planning a house together—planning a future.

Epilogue
SIX MONTHS LATER - MIRANDA

There are a lot of people who don't put much stock in the Farmer's Almanac, and I can see how they might think it's a little superstitious, based on wives' tales and moon phases. But it also seems to be right a lot of the time, and when Dad said the book predicted a snowy winter, it was right.

The first flakes began to drift down from between the huge red trees of our village in early December, coating the ground in a soft white blanket that didn't impede driving—or progress on Mr. Allen's cabin, which I'd personally done my very best to reprioritize so that Chance's promise of having it done by Christmas might come true. After a summer filled with flames and fear, even a little snow felt like a miracle, the cool white flakes soothing the fire scars of our village like a healing balm. Chance and Sam hadn't begun work on their new houses yet (Mr. Allen's had to get done first—I made them promise), but plans were finalized and they were going to be amazing. I'd personally picked out almost every major interior feature, and couldn't wait to see it all put in place. Chance had watched me work with Sam to design the house that I hoped I might share with him one day, and had asked if I'd do the interiors for his as well, and I'd agreed.

"Who knew you had all this talent in you?" Chance asked as I'd showed him my drawings for his new house.

From the other room, Sam shouted, "I did!" And I glowed. Sam's deep rich voice, always full of support and admiration for me, never got old. And now that we'd had time to explore the love between us, I knew he was telling the truth. Sam had always believed in me, always thought the best of me, even when I was pouring hot soup into his brother's lap at the diner because of my misplaced crush and stupid nerves.

"I guess that's why we put your name on the door, huh?" Chance said, coming out of his office and then smiling at me and giving my shoulder a squeeze.

I grinned. I still couldn't get over the changes in my life. As soon as I'd graduated with my degree, I'd arrived at work to find Sam and Chance both grinning madly at me and acting strange. They'd both looked weirdly nervous, and of course that had made me nervous. Once I'd finished tripping and flailing that morning, they'd sat me down and asked if I'd want to be a third partner in the business, handling the interior design aspect of our home building projects. The answer was easy for me, and it led to the name on the door of the office getting changed to Palmer and George Construction. My heart swelled every time I walked through that door, and one of the most gratifying things about my new position—besides the fact that I finally felt like a grownup—was the ability to refer jobs to my mom sometimes. Her business had boomed, too. It looked to be a good year for the George girls.

Soon after the fire, Cameron Turner had come into the office and offered his guest house to Chance and Sam as an alternative to living at the Inn until their homes could be built, and even though Sam was eager to have his own place, they accepted. I was still living with my parents, but I didn't mind. I felt lucky to have them both in my life, and to have them so close. In fact, Chance and Sam had both begun spending a couple evenings a week at my house just like they had when we were kids and our parents were all friends. In some ways I felt like I was sharing my parents with them, since they'd lost theirs. It was crowded in our little living room once the Palmer brothers with their long legs and wide smiles filled the space, but I don't think my parents minded any more than I did. Plus, I helped free up seating by perching myself on Sam's lap most of the time.

It was bizarre—the boy I'd actively worked to hate was the easiest man in the world to love. Sam Palmer was kind and thoughtful, funny and wise. And it had occurred to me more than once that all the things I'd thought I'd hated about him were things I actually loved. He was my steady solid point in a world that shifted quickly. He was like one of the huge big trees that surrounded my home. They stood, no matter what triumphs and tragedies were wrought by the tiny humans who played at their feet. Through thousands of years, they stood witness. If the fire had taken our town, those trees would have stood silently through the turmoil, coming out blackened but unhurt on the other side, steadfastly holding their position on this Earth and marking the passage of another era of humanity. Sam was like that. Less woody and more mobile, but a lot like one of those steadfast trees.

The Palmers were at my house for dinner the night the snow began falling around the village, and after we'd all stood out and marveled at the beauty of it, we'd gone back in to work on the puzzle we'd just started in the middle of our dining table.

"Think Mr. Allen's house can still be done in time for Christmas?" I asked Sam and Chance.

Chance whistled long and low. "You told me it had to be done."

Sam smiled at me. I'd become the conversational conduit between him and his brother, and in some ways I'd begun to run the office. Chance didn't make promises to clients without checking the schedule with me first, and Sam was much calmer now that Chance wasn't overpromising.

"I'd really like us to be able to keep the promise you made him," I said.

"Miranda," Chance began. "Construction is not about promises. It's about schedules, and those are often impacted by—"

"So we'll have it done?" I interrupted.

"If the snow's not too heavy, we'll get it done," he said, shaking his head at me.

My mother wore an almost-constant smile these days, and she looked up at me to smile now, something different lighting her eyes that made me a little bit nervous. Dad had been quiet all night, and Sam had been a little jumpy, standing up often and shaking out his newspaper while he looked around the room, as if expecting something to happen.

As I put in a piece of the puzzle, I felt Sam's gaze lingering on me and I looked up. He was staring at me, a warm look on his face and a tiny smile on his full lips that made my insides flip. I wanted to kiss that smile and watch it grow. I wanted to do lots of other things, too. I suddenly wished Sam and I could have a little time alone.

"Miranda," he said, reading my mind. "Take a walk with me?"

My mother let out a strange little yelp, and I looked at her questioningly.

"Excuse me," she chirped, covering her mouth with her hand as if she'd burped.

"Sure," I said, standing up. "Let me grab my coat."

We went out onto the porch, my parents and Chance watching us with more interest than normal, and I had a sneaking suspicion that something was afoot. The light from the house cast a warm glow around the structure, and it made the thin layer of snow that had fallen turn a soft yellow. The woodsmoke in the air was a comfort—fireplace fires smelled completely different from forest fires—and my heart swelled in my chest as Sam took my hand. My life had turned around so significantly in a short amount of time, I didn't know how much more happiness I could handle.

I let Sam lead me out into the darkness of the road, and we ambled slowly along, breathing the cold air. Sam put our clasped hands into the pocket of his warm coat and stopped walking, turning so we were facing one another.

"Remember when I went to a meeting at lunch today?" he asked without preamble.

"Yes," I said, wondering where he was going with this.

"Do you know who I met with?"

"The schedule said, 'important meeting,' and since you wouldn't let me come, I have no clue." There was a slight pout in my voice. I'd been a much bigger part of the business since becoming partner, and I didn't like being left out.

He chuckled, and the sound stirred the desire I'd felt inside. I rose up on my toes to kiss him. A little groan escaped his lips when I did, and he pulled me close and kissed me back. After a minute, he pulled away, his eyes on the cabin at the end of the road—Mrs. Teague's place. "You know what?" he said. "Would you mind taking a super quick detour?"

I held his hand and let him guide me as we walked to the widow's front door and knocked. I spoke to Mrs. Teague now and then, but I'd never dropped by unexpected. I grinned up at Sam. "What are we doing?"

"Just checking in," he said.

The old woman opened the door, looking small and a little bit frightened, but her face cleared when she saw Sam standing in the circle of light on her front doorstep. As soon as she recognized him, her hand went to her hair. "Oh hello, Sam," she said, and I would've sworn she blushed. "What are you doing here so late at night? Hello Miranda." Her eyes darted toward me, but then went right back to Sam, full of admiration.

"I just wanted to check in and say hello," he said. "I told you the other day I'd stop by again soon."

She smiled and then looked over at me, almost sheepishly. "Sam's been keeping me company lately, playing backgammon."

I smiled up at him. I knew we'd agreed to refinish her second floor, but I'd had no idea Sam and Mrs. Teague were friends.

"I just like to make sure you're happy and healthy," he said, his smile wide and warm. "And I wanted to see if we were still on for a walk tomorrow afternoon. Do you have snow boots?"

She gazed past us, maybe noticing the snow for the first time. "Oh my," she said. "I think I do have. I guess I'd better find them."

"Good," Sam said. "I'll be here at ten, and we can double check your heaters and make sure you've got plenty of firewood stacked where you can get to it easily, okay?"

My heart warmed as the woman's face glowed, and I couldn't help but feel proud of the man standing next to me, proud to be holding his hand. He was thoughtful and kind, warm and strong. And the way his eyes crinkled at the corners as he grinned at the old woman with genuine warmth lit another little flame inside me. Sam was a good man. In every way.

"I'll see you tomorrow Sam," Mrs. Teague said, her smile relaxed and happy.

"Good night," Sam and I both said, and we walked away after Mrs. Teague had closed her door.

I pressed myself against Sam's warm side, unable to stop myself from smiling. "You're a good man, Sam."

"Because I worry about an old lady on her own?"

"Yeah. That and about a million other things."

Sam stopped us then and took my other hand so I was facing him, the moon casting long blue shadows on the snow beginning to gather at our feet. "Do you know who I met with today?"

This again? "No," I said. "Are you going to tell me?"

"I met with your parents," he said.

What? Confusion swirled within my mind. "Are they building something?" It was odd they wouldn't mention it to me first.

"No, but maybe we are," he said.

Riddles were not my strong suit. "What are you talking about?"

Sam took both my hands in his and kissed each of my palms before wrapping my hands in the warmth of his bigger ones. Then he dropped to his knee in the gathering snow.

"Sam!" I laughed, half of me realizing what might be happening, and the other part still disbelieving and thinking only about how his knees were getting wet.

"Miranda," he said, his voice low and reverent. "I've loved you as long as I can remember. And I know we haven't been together a long time—as a couple I mean. But I know you like I know my own soul, and you know me better than anyone else. And you love me anyway."

"I do," I said, feeling the irony of the words as tears sprang to my eyes. "Even though you always smell like licorice."

"Shut up, you love it."

"I don't think you're supposed to tell me to shut up while you're proposing."

Sam grinned at me. "How do you know I'm proposing?"

Oh crap. I pulled my hands back, feeling silly. "You're not?

I mean … you had a meeting with my parents! What was—" My voice was rising quickly.

Sam took my hands back in his own. "Calm down," he said. "Let me finish."

I took a deep breath but couldn't help myself. "But are you proposing or not?"

"Miranda," Sam's voice held a little note of warning.

I shifted my weight impatiently. "Okay, okay. Sorry."

"Your parents gave me permission to speak to you tonight, to ask you a question."

"Yes." Excitement flooded my chest. He *was* proposing!

"I wondered if you'd do me the great honor—" his voice faltered slightly.

"Yes!" I was trying to make this easier for him.

"Of finishing this walk with me." He stood up.

"Wait, what?" My heart fell. "Walk? I don't …" What the hell? Had I been completely wrong about what was happening here?

Sam didn't say a word, but he didn't move either. "Dammit, Miranda," he finally said, turning to me. "I'm supposed to get to talk, and then once I've asked the question, you answer. That's how it's gone in my head every time."

The snow was falling thick around us now, and the confusion cleared. He *was* trying to propose. But I kept screwing it up. I nodded eagerly. "I'll be quiet."

Sam took to his knees again. "Miranda, you already make me happier every day than I knew I could ever be. Would you consider making me the happiest man in the world and become my wife?" He reached into his pocket and pulled out a little box, flipping open the lid. In the relative darkness, I couldn't see the color of the box, and I couldn't really see the ring, but the lights from my distant house reflected in Sam's eyes and glinted off the surface of the stone on the ring. I didn't care if it was tiny, I didn't care if it was a rock he'd picked up on the side of the road. What the ring looked like didn't matter at all to me. What mattered was the man before me, kneeling in the snow and asking if I'd spend my life with him. Tears rolled fat and happy down my cheeks and my chest squeezed with emotion.

"Yes," I said softly, dropping to my knees to face him. "Yes, I want to marry you," I said, and Sam threw his arms around me, pulling me close and pressing his lips to mine. He kissed me deeply and passionately, and I wasn't sure if hours went by or merely minutes, as heavy flakes of snow drifted down around us and Sam held me in his arms beneath the shadows of the trees that had witnessed every important moment in my life. Here was one more event for the Giant Sequoias to chronicle—the night I agreed to become Mrs. Sam Palmer as snow fell all around us in Kings Grove. The night my heart became fuller than I'd ever known it could be, and everything that had ever seemed wrong suddenly felt completely right. "I love you, Sam."

"Miranda," he said, slipping the ring onto my finger, "I love you more than you will ever know."

And in the presence of those big trees, atop a blanket of freshly fallen snow, my life began again.

THE END

Also by Delancey Stewart

Want more? Get early releases, sneak peeks and freebies! Join my mailing list at delanceystewart.com and get a free Mr. Match prequel novella!

The Singletree Series:

Happily Ever His

Happily Ever Hers

Shaking the Sleigh

Second Chance Spring

The MR. MATCH Series:

Book One: Scoring the Keeper's Sister

Book Two: Scoring a Fake Fiancée

Book Three: Scoring a Prince

Book Four: Scoring with the Boss

The Kings Grove Series:

When We Let Go

Open Your Eyes

The STARR RANCH WINERY Series:

Chasing a Starr

THE GIRLFRIENDS OF GOTHAM Series:

Men and Martinis

Highballs in the Hamptons

Cosmos and Commitment

The Girlfriends of Gotham Box Set

STANDALONES:

Let it Snow

Without Words

Without Promises

Mr. Big

Adagio

The **PROHIBITED!** Duet:

Prohibited!

The Glittering Life of Evie Mckenzie

CPSIA information can be obtained
at www.ICGtesting.com
Printed in the USA
BVHW041605110520
579510BV00003B/236